# QUEENS OF CYBERSPACE

## EXPANSION PACK

*Clancy Teitelbaum*

**E**
EPIC
Press

Expansion Pack
Queens of Cyberspace: Book #2

Written by Clancy Teitelbaum

Copyright © 2016 by Abdo Consulting Group, Inc.

Published by EPIC Press™
PO Box 398166
Minneapolis, MN 55439

All rights reserved.

Printed in the United States of America.

Cover design by Laura Mitchell
Images for cover art obtained from iStockPhoto.com
Edited by Jennifer Skogen

Library of Congress Cataloging-in-Publication Data

Teitelbaum, Clancy.
Expansion pack / Clancy Teitelbaum.
p. cm. — (Queens of cyberspace; #2)
Summary: Trapped in Io and betrayed by Ramses, the king of Altair, Brit, Mikayla,
and Suzanne flee to the queendom of Pyxis. While they travel through the game
world, they learn that even though Io is a fantasy world, its citizens face very real
problems—still, no matter how authentic Io feels to them, the girls can't forget
about their bodies waiting back in the real world.
ISBN 978-1-68076-198-6 (hardcover)
1. Friendship—Fiction. 2. Computer games—Fiction. 3. Internet—Fiction. 4.
Virtual reality—Fiction. 5. Cyberspace—Fiction. 6. Video games—Fiction. 7.
Young adult fiction. I. Title.
[Fic]—dc23
2015949424

*For sister A. and brother E.*

# Chapter 1

Suzanne didn't know what she had been expecting, but it certainly wasn't this. For three days she had been locked in a cell with her two best friends, Brit and Mikayla. While designing Io, the virtual reality that was everything and everywhere around them, Suzanne imagined a world of adventure for her friends. She didn't think they'd spend half a week locked in a dungeon waiting for a trial.

When the day of the trial came, Suzanne, Brit, and Mikayla were led from their cell through the lofty hallways of Zenith Castle. Their hands were in shackles and their feet bound together by a thick chain. That was enough restraint for Mikayla and Suzanne, but Brit's arms were tightly bound to her sides by chains thicker than Suzanne's hand. A dozen high-leveled Zenith City guards escorted them to the throne room, where the trial was to be held. The leader of the guards, a massive Dragoon, disengaged the Energite lock on the doors and flung them wide open, revealing the crowds within.

The room fell silent as the girls entered. The last time Suzanne was in the throne room, Ramses had charged the girls to kill a monster. Now he was charging the girls with murder and treason.

The lead guard tugged on their leg-chain, and the girls stumbled into a walk. Hundreds of NPCs sat, crowded into platform seats which graduated toward the ceiling. Suzanne wondered if Ramses had charged admission—he would have made a killing on ticket sales.

Suzanne wished she could pull up the hood on her cloak, but it had been confiscated with the rest of their armor when the Altairi Army captured the girls. She wasn't used to being the center of attention and could feel the NPCs' stares burning into her from all sides. The buzz of chatter filled the room, echoing off the vaulted ceiling. Suzanne wondered if any other trial in Altairi history had been so well attended. Then she wondered if there had been any other trials in Altair, period.

In the rear of the room was Ramses's magnificent throne. It was empty, as the king had not yet arrived. A plain table and three simples chairs occupied the center of the room. The guards led them toward the table, always making sure to keep their distance. The guards had kept their distance the entire journey to the throne room.

Suzanne supposed that made sense. After all, the girls were allegedly dangerous murderers. She didn't know about the murderer part, but dangerous? That was definitely true.

Suzanne scanned the crowd, looking for a friendly face. Whenever she managed to catch an

NPC's eye, the NPC looked away quickly. She saw a couple of Paladins and the odd Archer, but the NPCs assembled were predominately Citizens. They were dressed in the normal finery for Zenith citizens. The only Citizens Suzanne knew lived in the suburbs of Zenith City and couldn't have bought such nice items if they had liquidated their entire inventories.

They reached the benches. The guards waited for them to sit and then fastened the leg-chain through an iron rung in the floor. Suzanne saw the lead guard exhale a sigh of relief once the girls were fastened in, and the rest of the guards retreated a safe distance away to wait.

They didn't have to wait long. The doors creaked open again, and again the crowd fell silent. Suzanne turned to see a short, stocky, bald NPC, dressed in flowing gray robes, glide into the room.

"Who is it?" Brit asked. She was so heavily bound that she couldn't even turn around.

"Burgrave," Mikayla whispered. Brit made an angry sound.

As he neared the guards they stiffened into salutes. Burgrave nodded to them and they relaxed. He walked past the girls as if they weren't there, taking his place by the right hand of Ramses's throne.

After Burgrave, another NPC entered the hall. In a booming voice, the herald proclaimed, "Rise for your king and sovereign, Ramses of Altair!"

The hundreds of NPCs sounded like a stampede as they stood. But as soon as they had risen, silence reigned as King Ramses strode into the hall.

Ramses passed by the girls, a sneer on his face. The king's expression confirmed Suzanne's suspicion that this trial was going to be anything but fair. It looked like the girls were going to have to go with Plan B.

He ignored the death stare from Brit, his eyes fixed somewhere over the girls' heads. Without saying anything, he communicated what he really thought: that the girls were beneath him, that he was king, and this was his kingdom. Suzanne had never hated anyone more, human or NPC.

He climbed the steps to his throne, depositing himself in the gilded seat. The crowd sat back down as well, settling in for the trial.

"Brit, Mikayla, and Suzanne," the king said, letting his edged, icy voice linger on every syllable, "you stand charged of multiple counts of murder, of treason, and crimes against the crown. How do you plead?"

Brit strained against her chains, ready to fire off an angry retort. Mikayla placed a hand on her shoulder. While being transported to court, the girls discussed that Mikayla should do the talking.

Mikayla rose. She looked the king right in the eyes and said, "Not guilty."

The crowd immediately broke into loud whispers. Suzanne rolled her eyes. The crowd would have reacted like that no matter what Mikayla said. Ramses waited for quiet before he spoke again.

"Then we shall proceed with the trial. The evidence against the accused?"

Burgrave stepped forward from beside the king's right hand and withdrew from his inventory a broadsword. He laid it flat on the table in front of the three girls.

"Do you recognize this weapon?" the king asked.

"Yes," Mikayla said. The girls decided that the best way to approach the trial was to be as honest as possible.

"It belonged to Eirik, a commander in the Altairi Army," she added.

"If it belonged to Eirik, then may I ask how it came to be in Brit's possession?"

"We found it in the Lamia's caves," Mikayla said, which was true. They had stumbled upon the sword in the winding darkness of the Lamia's layer. The girls hadn't known Eirik for long, but he was a boisterous and likeable NPC. He wasn't the type to let go of his sword willingly. Brit had taken the sword with her so it could be returned to the Altairi Army, but they had been arrested before she had a chance to explain herself.

Mikayla explained as much to Ramses, but the king barely seemed to be listening.

"A wonderful story," the king replied. "I assume you have a similar explanation for why you killed Corvus and the rest of Eirik's unit?"

"Do you mean the Mongrels?" Mikayla asked.

The crowd broke out into whispers again. Suzanne knew what the mutterings were about. The girls had first met Corvus and his lackeys while the Mongrels were burning down the village of Oppold. They had been as surprised as anyone to learn that the raiders were part of the Altairi armed forces. Many in the crowd were refugees from towns like Oppold; even if they didn't know Corvus's name, they undoubtedly had heard of the Mongrels.

"If that's who you're talking about, then it was self-defense. They attacked us while we were leaving the dungeon."

"So you admit you killed them," the king replied.

"They didn't leave us a choice!" Brit shouted, unable to contain herself. "They were going to kill us!"

Suzanne whispered a caution to Brit, but her words were lost as the king began speaking again.

"It's convenient they aren't here to defend themselves, so that all we have to go on is the word of you three foreigners." His tone made it sound like being a foreigner was also a crime. "Where is it, again, that the three of you hail from?"

"From another land," Mikayla replied.

"From Pyxis?" Pyxis was the other nation in Io, currently at war with Altair.

"Your majesty," Burgrave said. "I have already told you that the girls are from neither Altair nor Pyxis."

Mikayla and Suzanne exchanged bewildered looks. Why was Burgrave standing up for them now?

"Ah, but Burgrave, you may have been deceived," the king said, not even looking at the official. Burgrave did not protest. He took the sword off the table and returned it to his inventory.

"Please, your majesty," Mikayla said, struggling to keep an ounce of respect in her tone. "We come from a land called Baltimore."

The crowd broke out into more whispers.

Ramses motioned to the guards, who banged their spears on the ground until the crowd was quiet. "Where is this Baltimore?" he demanded of the girls.

The three of them exchanged a look.

"We don't know where it is in relation to here," Mikayla replied.

The king sighed impatiently. "You admit you killed Corvus, yet you claim it was in self-defense. You say you are from this Baltimore, but cannot say where it is. I am beginning to wonder if you have answers that are possible to prove."

"We can prove what we are saying," Suzanne

said, rising. "We were fighting along three others—Picciotto, Desmond, and Samara, who saw the Mongrels attack us, and they were with us when we found Eirik's sword."

King Ramses fixed her with a look of disgust. "The three you spoke of fled as soon as you were arrested. Convenient that they are also not here to corroborate your claims, no?"

Suzanne sat back down, deflated. Picciotto's testimony would have cleared the girls, assuming the King accepted it as true. It made sense that he and his friends would flee once the girls were arrested. They were mercenaries, bound to sell their skills for coins, and sticking around would have been a very bad business decision.

"Assuming there is no more testimony you would like to submit, then I am ready to make my sentence."

"Wait!" Mikayla said. "There is someone else. Burgrave."

All eyes in the room turned toward the official.

Burgrave looked up toward the king, who nodded. Mikayla stepped past Suzanne, who scooted over toward Brit to make space.

"So, um," Mikayla said, pausing to clear her throat with a little cough. That was the signal. The girls didn't seriously think they would get a fair trial from Ramses, so they had come up with a backup plan just in case his sense of justice was as crooked as everything else about the king. Trying her best to look like she was following the trial, Suzanne began to pick the lock on Brit's chains.

Her hands were bound, but that didn't matter. Suzanne's class was a Rogue, and as a Rogue, she could pick locks. In the real world, the fact that her hands were chained together would have made the task a lot harder, but in Io lock-picking was simply a matter of solving a small sliding-block puzzle. And sure, it was harder to do the puzzle without looking at it, but Suzanne was the kind of girl who solved Rubik's Cubes while blindfolded for fun. The locks didn't stand a chance.

Brit strained against her chains, sensing she would soon be unfettered. Suzanne had to poke her in the side to remind her to stay calm. Once she felt the click of the first lock come undone, she moved on to the second.

"So you, um, met us outside Zenith City," Mikayla said.

Suzanne hoped that the king wouldn't notice Mikayla was stalling. But even more than that, she hoped Burgrave was sufficiently distracted by Mikayla's questioning that he wouldn't notice her picking the locks. Burgrave, like Mikayla, belonged to the Ranger family of classes. And while Rogues could pick locks, Rangers had improved awareness. Mikayla could see twice as far as Suzanne or Brit in game, but Burgrave's abilities were off the charts, completely without precedent. The plan depended on Mikayla holding his attention and Suzanne working extremely fast.

In another moment Brit's locks were completely undone. Brit coughed this time, signaling to Mikayla.

"Did you know that the Mongrels were raiding villages in Altair?" Mikayla asked Burgrave.

The official's reply was lost in the murmurs of the crowd. Ramses nodded to the guards standing behind the girls, who rapped their weapons on the floor to silence the crowd. Suzanne took the opportunity to undo the locks on her shackles and on the chains binding her feet. Lucky for her, if she kept her hands on her lap they would be close enough to her ankles to trigger the lock-picking game.

"Would you repeat yourself, Burgrave?" the king asked.

The official looked up at his king. "As I said, your majesty, I had no knowledge of such activities being undertaken by any members of the army. But I must confess that I had not met the soldiers that Mikayla refers to as the Mongrels prior to the expedition, and so I cannot vouch for their character."

"Whether or not you can vouch for the departed

is not the matter at hand," the king said. "What matters is if you can substantiate the claims made by the prisoner, and you cannot, so I thank you for your time."

"I see," the official said. Suzanne thought she saw a flicker of annoyance cross his face as he returned to his place by the king's side. Mikayla returned to her seat.

"Now you three," Ramses said, turning in his seat to face the girls. "You have claimed innocence, yet failed to provide any evidence. I find you guilty on all counts of murder and treason."

The crowd was completely silent now. All eyes were on the king, who was gloating in his triumph.

"Well I find you to be an asshole," Brit said, standing up. The unlocked chains slid off her body. Brit was a Fighter, the strongest of all the initial classes. With a grunt, she lifted the table over her head and threw it at the king.

Burgrave drew a scimitar from his robes and threw himself in front of the table. With a deft stroke, he slashed the table in half. The half tables crashed onto the floor, exploding into pixels. But in that moment, Brit grabbed the still-chained Mikayla and bowled through the awestruck guards, Suzanne following right behind them.

The tension in the room burst; the crowd erupted into panic. Half the Citizens struggled to flee the room, while the other half struggled to get as far away from the girls as possible. The chaos resulted in some NPCs falling down the stands.

Suzanne heard Ramses shouting orders to the guards above the chaos. But there was now a wall of NPCs between the guards and the girls. Brit reached the doors without slowing, charging through them like a battering ram.

Through the castle corridors they sped, Mikayla shouting directions at each turn. The hallways were mostly empty; the entire castle had been at the trial. The few Citizens who hadn't attended took one look at the fleeing convicts and threw themselves out of the way.

"You realize they'll never believe we're innocent now," Suzanne shouted.

"Fuck 'em," Brit said, her face composed in a wild grin. She was laughing with an exuberance that only freedom could bring.

# Chapter 2

Suzanne walked quickly through the Zenith City bazaar, her eyes on the ground to avoid any unwanted eye contact. In a way, it was like her first weeks of high school all over again. Except back then if anyone spotted her, it was likely just a bully trying to screw with her, and if anyone spotted her now, she'd be thrown back into prison.

It was funny; in those days Suzanne would have given anything to be invisible, and now, thanks to another of the Rogue class's special abilities, she basically was. Once she used Shadow Walk, most NPCs would ignore her unless she bumped into them or made direct eye contact.

A little timer appeared in the bottom-left corner of Suzanne's display. Once the numbers ran down to zero, her Shadow Walk would end and the cooldown period would begin, which marked how long before she could use the move again.

Despite the fact that it was thousands of feet in the air, Zenith City was filled with NPCs shopping and swapping items. Suzanne kept to the edges of the bazaar where there were fewer NPCs. Finally, after skirting a group of street performers who were juggling axes, she found what she was looking for: a merchant stall that sold normal armor as opposed to the enameled foppery most Zenith Citizens favored. Even better, the merchant was involved in a heated argument over the price of some daggers, not watching the items hanging on display.

She slowed her pace to a stroll. As she passed the stall, she brushed into three suits of caravan leather, a basic item that any class could wear. Instantly they vanished and entered her inventory—another of the Rogue's special talents was a heightened Theft ability. Once clear of the cart, Suzanne checked to see if the merchant had noticed, but the Shadow Walk had done its trick. The NPC was still haggling over weapons and hadn't noticed her wares were missing.

Suzanne ducked down an alleyway, leaving behind the crowds and dropping her Shadow Walk to preserve her Energite. Sticking mostly to side streets, she worked her way back toward the great elevators in Altair's central plaza. She fired off another Shadow Walk to cross the plaza, which was crowded with Citizens as well as soldiers no doubt on the lookout for the girls. But the Shadow Walk worked again and Suzanne made it safely back to the other girls' hiding place, an elaborate shrubbery.

"Took you long enough," Brit grumbled as she swapped her prisoner's clothing for the caravan leather.

Suzanne ignored her. "Did you find any merchants heading out of the city?"

"Yeah," Mikayla said. "But there are soldiers at the elevator checking all the carts before they let them on."

Suzanne thought for a moment. "What we need," she said, "is a diversion."

Minutes later everything was in place. Brit crept out from the shrubbery and got into position behind one of the merchant carts. She threw her body into it, sending it rolling into the middle of the plaza. Suzanne lobbed a Naphtha Bomb into the cart and watched as it burst into flames, scattering the nearby NPCs in terror. The cart rolled into another, spreading the blaze. The soldiers guarding the elevator swore and dashed off to help fight the flames.

Suzanne nailed the timing. No sooner had the guards run off than the elevator arrived. The merchants drove their carts on to the elevators in order to protect their precious cargo. But none of them noticed that in addition to swords and shields, they carried Brit, Mikayla, and Suzanne.

They held their breath as the elevator descended, waiting for soldiers to arrive and arrest them. But even when they were clear of the city, Mikayla insisted they stay hidden until the merchant stopped.

So they stewed in silence, the monotony only broken by the bumps in the road. The exhilaration of their escape couldn't sustain in such cramped quarters, and by the time they were finally rid of the merchant cart, their good mood from earlier had evaporated completely.

Suzanne passed the time by thinking about their situation. Even though they'd managed to escape from Zenith City, they were probably wanted throughout the kingdom of Altair. On top of that, their fugitive status all but ensured they wouldn't be able to use the hack point in Zenith Castle to log out. They might be free of Altair's prisons, but they were still trapped in the virtual world of Io, in a video game Suzanne herself had designed.

The merchant stopped for the night at an inn called The Hobgoblin's Hidey-Hole, located on the side of the Grand Highway. Suzanne found herself lusting after the rigid, uncomfortable NPC beds she knew would be in the inn. But as the girls walked from the stable toward the main building, Mikayla stopped in her tracks.

"Look," she said, pointing at a notice board.

Their faces were so poorly rendered that they looked like caricatures, but sure enough, pictures of all three girls, their mouths made up in cartoonish grimaces, glared down from the board.

Brit studied her portrait. "I didn't know I had such a savage unibrow."

"At least they spelled your name right," Mikayla said. "Honestly, who would think my name is spelled M-C-K-A-L-E-A?"

Suzanne wasn't looking at her picture, though it was hardly more flattering that Brit's. Her attention was focused mostly on the rather large sum being offered for her capture.

"Ten thousand gold," she muttered. "I guess they're pretty serious about recapturing us."

"Your bounty's ten thousand? Mine's only nine!" Brit looked so offended by the deficit that Suzanne couldn't help chuckling.

"It has our classes listed and everything," Mikayla said, still studying the notices. "Everyone's going to be looking for a Fighter, a Ranger, and a Rogue traveling together."

"We can't change our classes, can we?" Brit asked.

Suzanne shook her head, thinking. "Maybe we could pass for Citizens. You know, put our armor and weapons back in our inventories." The girls tried it, gesturing through their Menus to unequip their gear.

Without armor, Mikayla and Suzanne looked close enough to Citizens to avoid suspicion. Of course, there was the green icon floating over her head that marked her as a player character, but only the three girls were able to see that.

"Yeah, you two can definitely pass," said Brit, "but I don't think it's going to work as well for me."

Suzanne could see what she meant. Even without her armor, Brit's character was huge. No one would believe she was a Citizens, not when she was ducking through doorways.

"Maybe we're Citizens and you're our escort?" Mikayla suggested. "Or we could be merchants and we hired you for protection?"

They spent the next few minutes ironing the kinks out of their story. When Suzanne was confident their cover would hold, they walked from the stables to the main building of the inn.

Suzanne got the distinct impression that the inn was Io's equivalent of a motel. There were plenty of horses in the stables but their owners were already in bed. No doubt they would rise with the sun and be off along the highway on their business. That was good—if anything, they wanted to avoid busy spots. Besides the innkeeper, the merchant they'd

29

hitched a ride with, and a few mercenaries boasting drunkenly by the fire, the room was empty.

"How much for rooms?" Mikayla asked. The innkeeper held up four fingers. Suzanne handed over the gold and the innkeeper thrust a room key into her hand, all without saying a word.

"Friendly," Brit muttered as they walked past the bar toward the room. Her hand was on the door when one of the mercenaries, a Fencer, staggered to his feet and saluted the girls. He had a rather silly mustache and goatee and his long hair was tied in a ponytail. He wouldn't have been out of place at a renaissance fair in the real world. Suzanne wondered if he was as much of a douchebag as his appearance suggested.

"Hail the maidens fair!" he shouted, much to the delight of his comrades. Douche status confirmed.

"Ignore them," Suzanne said to Brit under her breath. Brit was gripping the doorknob so hard her fingers were beginning to depress the metal. The last thing they needed was to start trouble with a bunch of buffoons.

But the Fencer was not so easily satisfied.

"Pray tell, how did three ladies such as yourselves come to such a grim establishment as the Hobgoblin's?"

"We're merchants," Mikayla told him. "We were attacked by raiders and our Fighter managed to drive some of them off, but the rest of their band made off with our cart. We've been on foot since."

"How perfectly terrible," the Fencer crooned, stepping closer. "While I cannot offer compensation for your lost goods, I can certainly help you pass this cold night in comfort, warming your bed."

His comrades laughed even louder. Suzanne felt herself blushing.

"I don't think you could handle it," Mikayla said quietly. "Brit?"

With a flick of her wrist, Brit shoved the Fencer backwards. He stumbled over the legs of an Archer and nearly fell into a fire. The Fencer scrambled away from the embers. His comrades hooted with laughter.

"What do you think you're playing at?" he said angrily, but one withering look from Brit shut him right up.

Inside their room, Brit threw herself onto one of the cots, grimacing as the mattress refused to yield.

"So what now?" she asked.

Suzanne couldn't think of an answer before falling asleep.

She was woken hours later by a key fumbling in the door. "Hurry up," a voice hissed. Trying not to make any noise, Suzanne equipped her armor and weapons from her inventory.

Mikayla was already awake, her armor and weapons likewise ready. She was perched on her bed, her hand on her sword. In the third bed, Brit rolled over and snored loudly.

Whoever was trying to open the door stopped. Suzanne held her breath. She could imagine the intruder standing with their ear to the door, straining to hear any sign that the girls were awake. Brit snored again, which was apparently enough for the intruder. The key slid into the lock and opened with a click.

But whoever was behind the door didn't push it open. Mikayla slid back onto her bed and motioned for Suzanne to do the same.

She had barely settled herself when the door began to creak open. Doing their best to stay silent, the mercenaries from before filtered into the room.

"Told you it was them," the Archer whispered. In the dim light, Suzanne could just make out the notice for her arrest clutched in his hand. The Fencer from earlier must have been stalling them so the mercenaries could get a better look. No doubt they had sent word to the Altairi Army. *We need to get out of here*, Suzanne thought, *before the shit really hits the fan.*

Now that the mercenaries had gained entrance to the room, they seemed uncertain about what to do. They stood around awkwardly for a moment before the Fencer from earlier began to tiptoe across the room toward the beds.

Trying to stay as still as possible, Suzanne drew a dagger from its sheath. She waited until he was right in front of her and then stabbed at his stomach.

The dagger slipped under his breastplate— Suzanne felt the blade slide into his body—and the Fencer cried out in pain. With a soft popping sound, the dying Fencer burst into pixels. Suzanne was already up, another blade drawn, and she threw herself at the Archer who held up the arrest notice like a shield. Her daggers cut through the Archer as easily as the paper.

Mikayla launched herself from her bed and tackled another mercenary, a lanky Rogue, around the waist. He fell to the ground, his head smacking loudly on the floor. Mikayla finished him off with a thrust of her sword. She rolled his pixelating body into the doorway, trapping the other mercenaries inside.

"Get the fuck up, Brit!" she shouted. Brit snorted and sat upright in bed.

The remaining two mercenaries, another Archer and a Monk, cowered in the corner of the room. Brit set her feet on the ground heavily, and rubbed her temples.

"I just had the weirdest dream," she said.

"What?" Suzanne said. "You can't dream in the TII!"

Mikayla gave an exasperated sigh. "Can this wait? You're sleeping through these assholes trying to kill us."

"We weren't going to kill you," the Monk said, panic in his voice. He opened his mouth to say more but a glare from Mikayla shut him up.

"Sorry," Brit said, getting up and equipping her armor.

Suzanne walked across the room and held her dagger up to the Monk's throat.

"Did you call the army?" she demanded.

The Monk, scared silent, nodded frantically.

"When?"

"Uh, uh—about an hour ago," the Monk whimpered.

Mikayla walked over to the window and stuck her head out. "I don't hear anything yet, but that doesn't mean they aren't coming."

After a quick conference, the girls decided the best move would be to get going while they still could. They took the Monk and Archer's weapons and left them with the pixels of their fallen comrades.

The fire in the main room had gone out hours earlier. As the girls made their way through the darkened Hobgoblin's Hidey-Hole, the innkeeper launched himself over the bar.

"You aren't going anywhere," he said in his best intimidating growl.

Suzanne looked at the innkeeper with a mixture of frustration and pity. He was a Citizen; he could only make empty threats. Still, she was tired of NPCs fucking with her sleep schedule.

She strode across the main room and slapped the innkeeper in the face.

"Listen," she said, and the old NPC held his cheek and stared at her in fear. "We aren't fucking criminals. We didn't murder anyone. Your king is a douchebag and you're an idiot."

And with that, she turned and led the other girls out into the dawn.

# Chapter 3

"This armor is crap," Brit said. She slammed her halberd into a gila's spine, turning the lizard monster into a cloud of pixels.

Suzanne looked around to see that there were no more gilas. The dead monsters' pixels drifted upwards, disappearing into the leaves of the trees.

"It's better than nothing," Mikayla said, stooping to grab another monster's loot drop.

Brit scowled. "No shit. But there's a couple of degrees between nothing and something actually useful."

Suzanne rummaged through her inventory for a healing item. After the scrap in the Hobgoblin's

Hidey-Hole, the girls decided to stick to the woods and steer clear of NPCs. That meant no inns or merchants, no easy way to heal. They'd been surviving on the loot they got from killing monsters.

Suzanne found a Low Potion which materialized in her hand as a small jar. She walked over to Brit and used the potion on her. Brit's health bar flashed into view, expanding by a small chunk as the potion healed her.

Brit had to be healed first. As their front line, she was the one who took the most damage. But that didn't mean Mikayla and Suzanne weren't getting hurt, and they never had enough items to keep everyone healthy. It didn't really matter how much damage the girls took, as long as they had some health left.

And if all their health was gone . . . Suzanne didn't know what would happen then. She wasn't rushing to find out. Suzanne's best guess was that dying in-game would trap you in some kind of limbo. Without a body, you wouldn't be able to exist in Io, but the glitch wouldn't let you log out either.

But that wouldn't happen. Suzanne knew every monster in the world, so she knew what was coming. All they needed to do was get to Pyxis.

"This won't keep working," Mikayla said.

Brit laughed. "Allow me to repeat myself. No shit."

"It doesn't have to," Suzanne said. "We just have to make it to Pyxis. Then we can go to an inn and properly heal ourselves."

"I think we have to risk it," Mikayla said. "We need better armor, and we need to get our bearings. Like how are we even going to cross the river? Can our characters even swim?"

"Yeah," Brit said, joining in. "How do we know we won't find another village like Oppold where they don't give a shit about the king?"

"But if we get caught, we're screwed," Suzanne argued back.

"Maybe you're screwed, but I can take care of myself," Brit retorted.

Suzanne sighed. "No, you can't. Ramses has an army, remember?"

"Obviously we remember," Mikayla snapped. "Look, I get that this is your game and everything, but I don't think we're gonna make it to Pyxis like this. We need information, we need real armor, and we need to sleep in a bed."

"Look, I swear we'll make it, okay? But you and Brit can't stop and shop or sleep if we're going to keep our head start."

Mikayla put her hands on her hips, eyebrows arching in skepticism.

"What?" Suzanne asked.

"Are you sure we're going to make it to Pyxis? Just like how you were sure the TII was safe, and you were sure we'd be able to log out?"

"I don't know why any of that happened!" Suzanne yelled.

Mikayla shook her head. When she spoke, her

voice was impossibly calm. "You have no idea what's going on, do you?"

Suzanne couldn't answer. She had no idea Mikayla felt like that.

"Hey, whoa!" Brit cut in. "Why don't we scout out the next village we see? If it looks sketchy we skip it, but we might as well check it out."

Mikayla looked at Suzanne wordlessly for another moment before saying, "Whatever," and starting down the path. Brit gave Suzanne an apologetic shrug and hurried after Mikayla. Suzanne let herself trail behind them. She could hear them talking about something, but she couldn't make out their words. They were probably talking about her.

Brit hadn't looked surprised at Mikayla's outburst. Suzanne wondered if they'd been talking about her behind her back. All the time she was gone in Zenith City and when she went to sleep first in the inn—were Brit and Mikayla discussing how she'd fucked up?

Brit and Mikayla were closer with each other than either one was with Suzanne. And Suzanne knew that; she accepted it as part of the nature of their friendship. But that nature, that distance between them, was never so tangible before now.

At the next town they did what Brit said. Mikayla spotted a run-down sign for an equally run-down town called Reinke. There wasn't much town to speak of, just a few red brick buildings clustered together in a ditch beside a backwoods path leading to the Grand Highway.

But Suzanne thought Reinke was a good find. If they had to go into town, then a small town like this was much less likely to know about the girls and their fugitive status.

Brit had the most health, so she went to scope things out. Mikayla and Suzanne went to hide out in a ditch. Suzanne noticed that Mikayla was making a point of avoiding eye contact, her gaze turned toward the village, waiting for a sign from Brit.

Suzanne wasn't sure if she wanted to apologize to Mikayla or yell at her. She settled for slumping against a tree and breaking twigs, watching their pixels scatter.

It didn't help that she was tired. Mikayla was right, they did need to sleep in proper beds. The game made them tired at regular intervals, a sensation that wasn't eased unless an actual bed was slept in. Suzanne felt half-asleep all the time now. It made it hard to focus, and it was one more thing to change whenever they got out of Io.

"Do you hear that?" Mikayla asked.

Suzanne stopped breaking the twig and tried to hear what Mikayla was talking about, but all she heard were rustling leaves, muffled monster cries, and twittering birds. Normal sounds of the forest.

"What is it?" Suzanne whispered.

"Footsteps," Mikayla said, and she crept to the side of the ditch and drew her sword.

A minute later an NPC came running into view. He was sprinting full-speed away from Reinke.

The NPC was an Archer. He didn't have a bow or a quiver, but he did have a red character icon. NPCs only had red icons when they attacked one of the girls or an NPC in their party.

Suzanne realized what that meant just as the Archer sprinted past. She leapt up from the ditch and hurled a throwing knife, but she missed and the blade embedded in a tree trunk.

"What the hell?" Mikayla said, climbing out of the ditch.

"We have to help Brit!" Suzanne yelled. She began to run as fast as she could toward the village, and after a few seconds Mikayla caught up.

As they approached the village, Suzanne could hear the sounds of metal weapons clashing against armor. Without saying anything, Mikayla sped up, and Suzanne found herself falling a few steps behind. Soon they reached the wooden fence surrounding the village, the line that monsters couldn't cross. Suzanne heard a shout of pain and willed her legs to go faster.

They arrived in the small town square to see Brit facing off against a Sellsword. They were surrounded by Citizens and loot drops from other NPCs Brit had already taken out.

Brit charged at the Sellsword. He jabbed at her with his sword and Brit swung her halberd into his torso. The Sellsword pixelated. So did Brit's armor. She took an unsteady step and then crumpled to the ground.

"Brit!" Mikayla shouted. The Citizens scattered at the sight of more characters with weapons, clearing a path to where Brit lay. Dropping to her knees, Mikayla tried to shake Brit awake.

One of the Citizens, a man dressed in plain brown clothes, with an commonplace face— Suzanne recognized him as one of the generic Citizen designs—stepped forward.

"Are you friends of hers?" he asked.

Suzanne nodded.

"She defended us, but there were too many of them . . . " His voice trailed off.

Suzanne knelt beside Mikayla and used another low-potion on Brit. Brit's health-bar flashed back into view. The potion raised her health from three to fifty-three but Brit didn't stir.

"She's unconscious," Suzanne said, not fully believing the words. "She's lost too much health." But that shouldn't have knocked her out.

Mikayla was staring at Suzanne, her eyes wide with fear. Suzanne knew they were thinking the same thing. It shouldn't matter how much health you lost unless you lost all of it. What was going on?

"Where's the inn?" Suzanne asked the Citizen. He pointed toward a two-story building on the southern edge of the town square. Suzanne saw their WANTED posters hung up outside. She'd deal with that later. Right now they had other priorities.

"We need to move Brit," Suzanne said.

Jeremy, as the NPC identified himself, marshaled a group of Citizens to help lift Brit. While they moved her to the inn, he explained what had happened.

"We've been getting raiders from Pyxis for the last couple months. Of course we sent word to the king, but none came back. So when this crew showed up we got ready to lose all our valuables as usual.

"But then your friend showed up. I recognized her from the bounty posters. You two are Suzanne and Mikayla, right? Well, we all thought she was with the raiders, but she went right to town on them. One of them ran off, probably to get some more friends. There must have been half a dozen but she took them all down."

They had moved Brit up to a bed in the inn. Lying there, Suzanne couldn't help thinking that Brit looked like a body at an open-casket funeral. She was still, far too still. The rest of the Citizens filed out, leaving Jeremy with Suzanne, Mikayla, and the still unconscious Brit.

"I thought you three were enemies," Jeremy said. "The king's notice said you were."

Suzanne studied the NPC's face. He looked guilty, like he was the one who had hurt Brit.

"You didn't know," Mikayla told him stiffly. "Thank you for your help."

He bowed and left. Mikayla dragged a chair across the room and placed it next to the bed.

"He's going to report back to Ramses," Suzanne said. "That guy who ran past us."

Mikayla didn't look up. She hovered over Brit, holding herself back like she was afraid to touch their unconscious friend.

It was as if Suzanne wasn't in the room at all. She sat down on the other bed and waited for Brit to wake up.

# Chapter 4

N ear dawn, Suzanne woke up. She blinked a few times, adjusting to the gray light. The cell where she waited for trial had been washed in yellow candlelight. Suzanne felt the soft gray light calm her.

Mikayla had curled up next to her on the spare bed. Suzanne studied her for a moment. Mikayla's character, asleep, was peaceful. Suzanne felt a twinge of regret as she shook Mikayla awake, but it was time to move on.

"Is Brit . . . " Mikayla began asking. She didn't finish the sentence.

Brit lay inert on the main bed. Fully awake,

Mikayla's features rearranged themselves into worry. She looked drawn. Suzanne was hoping that was a trick of the light.

"We need to go." Suzanne surprised herself with the hardness in her voice. They burned all their time for wallowing in the night. The raider that survived Brit would have no doubt linked up with the main forces of Altair by now, and even though Suzanne wasn't looking forward to dragging Brit through the wilds, she knew they couldn't face the army.

In a flash, Mikayla was up, her armor and weapons equipped. They carried Brit downstairs, Mikayla holding her shoulders, and Suzanne, her legs. *Like she's a corpse*, Suzanne thought. She shuddered at the thought and her grip on Brit's ankle slipped. Unable to hold the weight by herself, Brit's body dragged Mikayla down the stairs. Suzanne jumped aside as Brit crashed to the bottom of the stairs.

The corner of Mikayla's mouth twitched.

Suzanne felt a bubble of laughter but she hiccuped it away.

Mikayla didn't ask why Brit hadn't woken up. She wouldn't take her eyes off Brit. She waited silently while Suzanne bought a cart from one of the NPCs. After they loaded Brit into the cart, Suzanne saw Mikayla brush Brit's hair out of her face. She felt like she should say something to Mikayla, but she was still afraid of Mikayla snapping at her again. She didn't want Mikayla to blame her for Brit along with everything else.

With Mikayla pushing and Suzanne pulling, they left the village of Reinke. They traveled down a well-worn forest path for a while in silence. Then, Mikayla said, "The army's going to be majorly pissed. They'll know those villagers helped us."

Suzanne didn't spare a thought for the NPCs. No doubt the army would be mad when they found out the girls had been there and they'd be furious at the NPCs for helping them. But they were only programs, and bland ones at that.

"That's how it works," she said. "You help someone out and everybody gets screwed."

"That's some bleak shit," Mikayla replied.

Suzanne chuckled. "Yeah, I guess it is."

They did their best to keep the cart steady, but the road was uneven. Despite the jostling, Brit remained conked out. By midday Reinke was out of sight behind them. It was early afternoon when they caught their first sight of the river.

Suzanne's heart sunk. In the map editor on her computer, back when she was designing the game, the Ion River was just a stretch of blue on a monitor, barely wider than the cursor of her mouse. She struggled to reconcile that thin blue line with the body of water in front of her.

"Let's get down to the bank," Suzanne said, her voice listless.

The road sloped downhill toward the bank. Wild grasses overtook the path, growing up to Suzanne's waist. Then there was water. A strong current dragged waves downstream. Tumbling over each other, they sprayed white foam in the air.

The Pyxian shore was a craggy bank off in the distance. Suzanne couldn't imagine a way to get across. She doubted Brit's cart could float, and even if it did, they had no way to fight the current. There were large waterbirds, wings folded in, floating along as if the water was placid. But it wasn't like Suzanne could just whistle and summon a flock to ferry them across.

Battle toads, which were amphibian monsters armed with slimy maces, croaked at each other as Suzanne and Mikayla shoved Brit's cart down to the shore, but they gave the girls a wide berth. Suzanne hadn't seen them in the TII yet, but she couldn't stop to check them out. They had to figure out a way to Pyxis before they were trapped between the river and the army on their tail.

From Mikayla came a sharp intake of breath. No doubt she was coming to the same conclusions.

Maybe her Ranger vision had shown her an answer to their predicament.

"Does it narrow anywhere?" Suzanne asked Mikayla.

"No," Mikayla said, her voice muffled and dull.

They pushed Brit's cart beneath the canopy of a tree and threw themselves down in the shade to think.

"Could we swim?"

Suzanne thought for a minute but shook her head *no*. "Our strength stat probably isn't high enough to get us across, and that's ignoring Brit."

Mikayla gazed at Brit and sighed. "If she was up she could just throw us across. Or knock down a tree or whatever."

Suzanne racked her brain, trying to figure out a way across the river. Maybe there was a fishing village nearby where they could hire a boat. But when she pulled her map out of her inventory and checked it, she couldn't find any villages within a day's walk of them. Burdened by Brit, the Altairis would catch up before they could reach help.

*Don't get frustrated*, Suzanne told herself. She sat and waited for inspiration to hit her.

It didn't. But an apple did.

The fruit bounced off her head and rolled over the grass, coming to rest a few feet away from Mikayla. She didn't notice as she was busy yanking up clumps of grass and watching it pixelate in her hand. Suzanne looked around but she couldn't see where the fruit would have come from.

A second apple flew at her. This time she saw it coming and ducked. It had come flying out of the bushes, not out of a tree. Someone had thrown it.

She drew her dagger and fired up a Shadow Walk. It was probably nothing, just some toads or swordsfish messing around, but it didn't hurt to take precautions. She crept toward the bushes, only pausing to avoid a third apple that came flying out of them.

Then she heard the voices whispering.

"You're such an idiot," a girl's voice said. Whoever she was, she sounded exasperated.

"What else are we going to do with all these apples?" The second voice was a boy's, and it sounded highly amused.

"It boggles the mind that we are related," the girl's voice replied. "If there weren't such strong evidence for it, I'd dismiss our siblinghood as a fiction."

The boy laughed pleasantly. Suzanne tried to part the bush. It rustled as she pried the foliage apart, but only a little.

Though partially obscured, she could make out the girl and boy standing behind the bushes. They were about the same height, with tawny hair. Suzanne thought she saw the girl glance toward the bush, but then her brother spoke again.

"Dear sister, I do not intend to row a boatful of apples to Pyxis. I know you delight in the flora of Altair, but there's no need for you to bring an entire orchard with us."

Another apple flew from behind the bushes. This time, Suzanne caught it. They had a boat, and they were going to Pyxis! All she had to do was convince them to take her and her friends along. And if they couldn't be convinced . . . She pulled a dagger off her belt and glanced down at the blade. She would just have to be more persuasive.

She looked back up. The siblings must have moved, because Suzanne could no longer see them. Trusting the Shadow Walk would cloak her, she stood up and stared over the hedge.

No one was there. There was a large rowboat nested in the roots of a tree, and it was filled with apples. But neither the boy nor the girl were anywhere to seen.

"Drop the dagger," the girl's voice said. Suzanne looked up and saw the girl balanced in the branches above her. The lightness had left her voice; it was now as sharp as the weapon aimed at Suzanne's head.

She looked like she was about Suzanne's age,

maybe a year older. Her hair was done up in a bun behind her head, held in shape by a slender knife. But Suzanne hardly noticed the girl. Her attention was mostly focused on the naginata in the girl's hand—a long pole with sword-blades fixed on both ends. Suzanne could see her reflection in the blade hovering a foot from her head. Something in her coal-black eyes said this girl wasn't fucking around.

"You might as well do what she says. It'd be a shame for you to get wasted over nothing."

She turned around and saw the boy. He looked around the same age as his sister, tall and broad. He was built like a soccer player, all lean muscle and easy confidence. He held a stave with an iron ball for a cudgel.

He had unkempt, sandy hair and his eyes were an acute gray. He wore robes like his sister. Suzanne realized where she had seen robes like this before: Burgrave, the chief official in the court of King Ramses.

"Are you from Pyxis?" she asked.

"Why ruin such a nice day with questions?" he replied.

"Please," Suzanne said, trying to keep her voice even. "My friends and I need to go there."

He studied her face, not saying anything. His gaze reminded Suzanne of the wide-eyed stare she'd gotten from Burgrave in the past, but Burgrave looked nothing like this NPC. The Altairi official was full of cold scrutiny, but the boy in front of her right now looked halfway amused.

After a minute he smiled and said, "Okay, we'll take you."

"What?" his sister shouted. "You have no idea who they are! For all you know they could be here to kill us!"

Suzanne didn't take her eyes off of the boy. Something about him was hypnotizing.

"Calm down," he said to his sister. His face broke out into a wide smile. "What's the worst that can happen?"

"We die, you nitwit," she retorted. "That's always the worst thing that can happen. We don't even know where her friends are or how many of them there are. Damn it, Leo, we don't even know why they want to go Pyxis in the first place!"

Leo shrugged. "Well I suppose we'll have to ask. Why don't you bring your friends back here and tell us your story?"

Suzanne found herself grinning as she dashed back toward Mikayla.

"What's going on?" Mikayla asked. She was crouched by Brit's cart, her sword in her hand.

Suzanne almost laughed at Mikayla's expression. "I found some people who can take across the river!" she crowed. After Suzanne explained, they wheeled Brit over to the siblings, who were still arguing.

"Just because you think she's pretty," Suzanne heard the girl saying.

"Oh come off it," Leo replied. "They need our

help!" Something about his tone told Suzanne that his sister's barb hit close to home.

"Hi," Suzanne said, pushing through the bushes.

Leo started and took a step back. "Stop sneaking up like that!" he laughed.

His sister resumed glaring at Suzanne.

"My name's Suzanne. This is my friend Mikayla," she said. Mikayla nodded and bowed slightly from the waist. "And that's our friend Brit. But she's hurt and she won't wake up."

"I'm Leo," the boy said, "And the sourpuss over there is my sister Lynx. But what's wrong with your friend?"

He walked over to Brit and examined her for a second before motioning his sister over. They conversed in hushed tones. Suzanne made a mental note to ask Mikayla what they had said later.

"Who did this to her?" Leo asked.

"Altairi soldiers," Mikayla said.

Lynx was still staring at Brit. "This is bad," she said. Seeing the concern on Suzanne and Mikayla's face, she added, "Oh, not your friend! She'll be fine. But if there are soldiers in Altair who can do this, that's bad."

Leo nodded and placed a hand on Brit's forehead. "Cleanse," he said. White rings surrounded his arm, flowing downward from his shoulder to his fingertips. They passed onto Brit's body, encircling her in a cocoon of white light. He's a War Priest, Suzanne realized. That was an advanced support class. You had to clear four specific quests before you could become a War Priest. Suzanne supposed an NPC could clear them, but she never imagined that one would. Just who were these siblings, exactly?

The rings dissipated. Brit coughed once and sat upright blinking.

"What's up?" she asked, a dazed smile on her face. Mikayla and Suzanne threw their arms around her, hugging her so hard that Brit had to push them off before she could speak.

"What happened?" Brit asked. "Last thing I

remember someone hit me with some kind of special attack, but it's all fuzzy after that."

"Someone inflicted you with Sleep," Leo said.

"Why didn't it wear off at the inn?" Mikayla asked, once the introductions were made. "We've been Poisoned and Hobbled before, but sleeping always fixed whatever status we had."

"There are monsters who inflict permanent status," Lynx said. "Poison that can't be cured, for example. You just waste away slowly until you are gone. Apparently Ramses learned some tricks from the foul things."

No one said anything. Suzanne wondered if Ramses had extracted those skills from the Oracle Chamber, too. Suddenly she was even happier to be leaving Altair behind.

"What are we waiting for?" Leo asked. "Let's get to Pyxis!"

# Chapter 5

Suzanne closed her eyes. She sat on the bow of Lynx and Leo's rowboat as it crossed the river. Leo steered the rudder and no one rowed—an advantage of boat travel in video games—but the journey wasn't instantaneous. And Suzanne, who had never been on a ship in the real world, couldn't believe how seasick she got while crossing the Ion River. She felt like someone was using her stomach as a baster.

No one else seemed to have much trouble with the crossing. Mikayla perched on the stern, bobbing and weaving with the ship. The wind whipped Suzanne's hair around her face. She envied Mikayla's short haircut.

Brit, already recovered from the Sleep, chatted with Lynx and Leo.

"We should form a party," Leo was saying. "It would make it easier for me to heal you three."

Suzanne tried to ignore her queasiness so she could listen. She was surprised that an NPC would suggest forming a party. As long as they were all in a party, Leo could split his healing abilities among them instead of healing them one at a time.

Their boat reached the Pyxian shore. They hiked up the embankment to see a vast savannah in front of them, with small groves of trees springing up from the earth. The air in Altair had been cool and crisp, but in Pyxis humidity pervaded every breath. The robes the Pyxians wore made a lot more sense. No doubt they were cooler than the Altairi armor the girls had equipped.

Brit clapped Suzanne on the back. "We made

it!" she beamed. The Sleep had left her no worse for the wear.

"No thanks to your snoring ass," Mikayla muttered.

Brit stuck her tongue out at Mikayla. "Whatever. At least we're safe now."

Of course, safety was merely relative. A pride of sabreclaws, huge wildcats with dusty coats, emerged from the savannah grasses.

The girls drew their weapons and stepped forward. Lynx produced her poled-blades and joined them, but Suzanne noticed Leo dropping back behind them. She didn't have time to reflect on that as a sabreclaw hurled itself at her, raking at her face with its needle-filled paws.

Suzanne leapt back and then forward, shoving her dagger into its neck. The cat beast mewled at her and expired, bursting into pixels. It dropped a few golden coins and cat's claws for loot.

Suzanne heard a roar and whirled to face another charging sabreclaw. But Lynx's knife whizzed past her, knocking the leaping creature out of the air. Lynx flashed Suzanne a smirk before whirling her pole-weapon to strike down another sabreclaw. Her hair splayed out, loose without the knife holding it in place.

Suzanne couldn't help being awed by Lynx's skills. Her fighting style was all about rhythm. She'd take a few steps back from her opponent and begin spinning her weapon, feinting and striking in time with the arc of the blades. The blades moved so fast that it looked like Lynx was striking from multiple places simultaneously.

More sabreclaws came growling out of the grass. A scarred male pounced at Suzanne. She rolled under it, but right into the paws of another. Her health bar dropped as razor-sharp claws slashed into her back. But just as quickly as it dropped, her health went back up.

She pushed the monster off her and finished it with two quick stabs. Leo stood a few feet away, the same white bands of light encircling his arms. Now they were wrapped around his staff as well, emanating out toward the rest of the party.

Abruptly, the white light vanished. Suzanne knew Leo would have to wait for his spell to cool down before he could heal the party again. That was the way it worked with Priests—while they weren't healing, they were sitting ducks.

But apparently Leo was no mere support character. Thinking him easy prey, a sabreclaw tried to attack him. But Leo charged straight toward the creature, before pivoting at the last moment and twirling his staff as he spun around it. He dealt the sabreclaw a blow in the back of the skull, knocking it toward his sister. As Lynx dispatched the monster with her whirling blades, Leo flashed Suzanne a smile.

Brit finished off the last sabreclaws with a two-handed blow.

"These monsters are a piece of cake," she said, reaching down to grab loot. Suzanne agreed that the fight hadn't been hard, but she wondered how things would've gone without Lynx and Leo.

After checking to make sure everyone was okay, the party set off. As they walked, Leo explained his people's side of the war.

"About a year or two back they showed up at the Capital," he said. "Ramses and his army. They demanded all sorts of things. They wanted to build a bridge across the river, which seemed reasonable enough. But what they really wanted was everything: our gold, our Energite, and our land."

Leo took a moment to master his anger before continuing. "We didn't have an army. You have to understand, we weren't expecting a war. None of us were fighters. The attack caught us entirely by surprise."

"It didn't take Ramses long to drive the queen out of the Capital. After that, they sacked Pyxia.

I haven't been back since we were forced to flee. I have no idea how much of my home remains."

He fell silent, and Lynx picked up the story.

"It didn't matter too much. Queen Libra and her court fled to the mountains in the west. Since then, she's been trying to rally an army, but it's been tough."

*So that's what they're up to,* Suzanne thought, remembering Leo's words about a mission earlier. But why hadn't they tried to recruit the girls? Maybe the Pyxians still didn't trust them. Suzanne didn't mind the idea of spending more time with Leo.

She also had to wonder where they were headed. Lynx led them forward without pausing to consult a map, always west. One stretch of savannah looked like all the others to her.

But Lynx evidently knew where she was going, because just as the sun set, they came upon a camp. Tents were set up in a series of concentric circles, ringing around a meeting area in the center.

Suzanne had been camping exactly once in her life. Her dad's flimsy tent hadn't kept out rain or bugs. The Pyxian tents were a far cry from that. Not only were they closer to mobile pavilions the size of cottages, but they also restored hit points while you slept in them, like a bed.

Lynx led the way into the camp, exchanging smiles and greetings with various NPCs that came out to greet them. Suzanne noticed that the NPCs, while polite, eyed her and her friends suspiciously. All the NPCs wore robes, so the girls' Altairi armor made them stick out. Suzanne understood why the Pyxians were wary, but it was still unsettling, feeling eyes on you every time you turned around.

Leo was greeted even more openly than Lynx. He broke away from the party to catch up with some of the NPCs. Lynx led the way through the tents to the center of the camp, where a fire blazed.

*Really*, Suzanne thought, *there are only two kinds of NPCs.* There were the myriad varieties—grouped by class, by age and complexion, gender and level and homeland and whatever. But all these distinctions mattered very little in the context of the great divide, between the intelligent and the not-so-much. Suzanne thought of them as the companions and the filler. She had noticed it before, how some NPCs had grey diamonds for their character icons and some had grey crowns.

The filler smiled pleasantly and had maybe six, maybe seven lines of dialogue. They were the majority. Merchants made good filler, as did children. Guards were excellent filler characters. The key was that the character needed an occupation that demanded very little of them verbally. So while it might behoove a guard to know more than a handful of phrases, it didn't matter terribly either way.

Lynx and Leo belonged firmly in the companion camp. The grey crowns twirling over their heads proved it. They had an easy fluency that elevated them above the filler NPCs. It was coupled with a natural air of command, and it drew the filler NPCs to them like magnets to metal.

Suzanne watched Leo as the camp gathered around the fire. He knew the name of every member of the camp, what they did, and what news might be most relevant to them. "Russell," he said, speaking to a long-haired Ranger. "Did you ever find that weremonkey that stole your hat?"

Russell smiled, said No, he hadn't, but he would keep looking.

That was all he had to say. But Leo didn't begrudge the other NPC that. He had a question for every Pyxian at the fire and every Pyxian passing by. His depth lay in their numbers. Lynx was like her brother, albeit slightly more reserved.

Suzanne had met other NPCs like the twins. King Ramses and Burgrave of Altair's government were both capable of the conversational complexity that Leo and Lynx assumed, as were Picciotto and Samara. But the companion NPCs they had met in Altair were regal or exclusive. Picciotto and

Samara hardly interacted with anyone outside of their group, and Ramses and Burgrave constantly maintained an air of superiority that meant they condescended to nearly everyone. Small talk, Suzanne realized, was a special ability in and of itself.

The NPCs broke out food and wine. Suzanne planned on skipping the booze but Lynx brought a bottle over to the girls and insisted. Like all the food in-game, it was a crude approximation of flavors. There was fruit, like grapes, but it lacked all the sourness that makes grapes refreshing. There were fresh-baked loaves of bread, but even though Suzanne had watched the NPCs pull them off the fire, they lacked the warmth of bread in the real world.

The wine, though, was excellent.

To be fair, Suzanne wasn't much of a drinker. But even Brit, who was known to spike punch bowls at dances, enjoyed the Pyxian wine. It was sweet without being cloying and it carried the suggestion of alcohol without the taste. Suzanne enjoyed it so much that she quickly drained her first glass, and then a second. Before long she, Brit, and Mikayla had drained a flagon between the three of them.

Suzanne set the bottle down and realized she was drunk. The edges of her vision had blurred and her character's response felt sluggish. It had happened all of a sudden, without a stopover in tipsy town.

"Brit!" she whispered, a little too loudly. Brit looked over with a dazed smile on her face.

"We're drunk." Suzanne felt it was urgent she told Brit this.

Brit nodded sagely. "You're drunk. I'm totally cool."

Suzanne's head bobbed vigorously up and down. "Very cool," she slurred.

Mikayla laughed until she snorted, slipping off her seat. All three of them laughed harder.

Across the fire, some of the Pyxians were staring. Self-consciousness flooded Suzanne until she noticed the stack of empties littered around their end of the fire. She had programmed the game so that every character had the same tolerance.

"Not bad?" Leo asked, strolling over. His smile seemed a little looser than usual.

"Great!" Brit shouted, breaking into more giggles.

He closed his eyes and nodded. "We wanted to welcome you to Pyxis properly. Show you that there's more to the kingdom than monsters and grass. Though there are plenty of monsters and grass."

Suzanne brushed her hair behind her ear, hoping it made her look more sober.

"May I ask what you plan on doing in Pyxis?" He was trying to be casual but his grey eyes had hardened with intensity.

Suzanne saw Lynx flicker to attention across the fire.

"We need to head to the Capital," she said.

"What for?"

"Sightseeing," Mikayla cut in. Leo's gaze shifted to her and Mikayla met his eyes fearlessly. Lynx watched intently. Was this why the twins had brought them to the camp? To get them drunk and question them?

Brit burped loudly, and everyone around the fire, player and NPC, companion and filler, laughed together.

One by one, the NPCs left the circle and stumbled off to their tents to sleep. The fire burned down to its embers as the crowd around it dwindled.

Suzanne felt sobriety right around the corner. She felt exhausted. That morning they had been in another kingdom with an army pursuing them.

Beside her Brit stretched and yawned, trundling off to find somewhere to pass out. Mikayla followed her back into the cluster of tents.

And then it was just Suzanne and Leo sitting around the fire.

Suzanne stared into the firepit, watching the

loop of animation. She had coded the way it crack-led, five seconds of flames. It helped her balance. But she realized Leo wasn't looking at the flames; he was looking at her. She met his gaze. His eyes caught the firelight and burned orange and gray.

"I wish . . . " he began. The words seemed to catch in his throat. He shook his head and looked away.

"What?" she asked.

He looked up at her and smiled. "I wish you'd tell me what you were really doing here. I wish you'd let me help you."

"Maybe you need our help," she muttered.

"Maybe we do," he said quietly.

"It's not just up to me. Mikayla and Brit, I owe them everything. I wouldn't have made it this long without them. But I wasn't fucking with you. We are headed to the Capital."

He stood and pointed off into the darkness. "Then head south," he said. "You're going to see a huge ridge where the grasslands drop off a cliff. That's where you'll find Pyxia."

He looked like he might say something more, but thought better of it. He made a few gestures with his hands, and Suzanne saw a small notification stating Leo and Lynx had left her party. Then the prince walked off.

The last embers died, leaving Suzanne to find her way to a tent in the darkness. When she woke in the morning, the twins were already gone.

# Chapter 6

"**F**ucking shit," Brit grumbled. Suzanne watched her sit up, holding her head in both hands. Considering the hangover she was dealing with, the effort was nothing short of herculean.

Suzanne was feeling like an idiot for putting hangovers in the game. She wanted to make Io as realistic as possible, but this was really pushing it. Besides a few times with Brit and Mikayla, she never drank in the real world. So Io's hangovers were as much guesswork as anything.

Suzanne woke with the bright light of morning scalding her eyes. The room wobbled before her. The act of seeing was making her nauseous. Opening her eyes more than a squint took a lot of willpower. Getting up would be asking for too much.

Brit didn't get further than sitting up. "Just kill me," she said. "Use some Energite and Backstab me to Hell."

She gave a feeble laugh and flopped back onto the sleeping mat. They lay there, dozing when the headaches and nausea would let them, for most of the morning.

Around noon, Mikayla came in.

"You can't still be sleeping."

"How are you moving?" Suzanne asked. "Special Ranger liver?"

"I'm just not a baby like the two of you."

"Funny," Brit said. "You hung onto that bottle like you were one."

"Yeah, well, who's the one too hung over to move?"

Suzanne laughed weakly. With a roar, Brit

threw herself out of bed. She swayed on her feet but stayed standing.

"Suck it," she said to Mikayla.

"I most certainly will not," Mikayla replied.

They advanced on Suzanne. Seeing what they intended, she pulled the blanket over her, as if it could shield herself from her friends.

"Come on, Suze," Brit said. "Time to get up."

She grabbed one arm and Mikayla grabbed the other. Together, they yanked her out from under the blanket. Suzanne was sore from sleeping in her armor and her headache still pounded. But Brit and Mikayla didn't let go of her arms. They dragged her out of the tent.

"We've got to go," Mikayla said. "They're packing up the camp."

All around them, NPCs were collapsing the tents and loading them onto the back of carts. The girls ran to the last open merchant and purchased three of the Pyxian tents. While Suzanne crammed her tent in her inventory, she saw Russell speaking with a group of armed NPCs.

"We're the Caravan Guards," he explained once the girls caught up with him. "By the way," he added, "Leo wanted me to tell you goodbye. Said he hopes to see you again."

"Thanks," Mikayla replied.

"You especially." He pointed right at Suzanne. Her stomach turned, and this time, it wasn't the aftereffects of last night's drinking.

"Course, he said to be clever with how I did it." Russell shrugged and trundled off.

The other girls gave her shit about it as they walked toward the Capital. Suzanne was used to this kind of teasing, although normally she was the one dishing it out rather than the one taking it. Back in the real world, Mikayla was the only one of them who did any dating. She'd suffered a series of mediocre relationships over the past two years. Brit never failed to point out the guy's obvious flaws, even after Mikayla broke it off.

There was Corey Jameson, the tight end for their school's football team. He was a nice enough guy, but seemed to think that sweatpants were the right piece of clothing to anchor a wardrobe around, and also that his didn't need washing. Tyler Huffman could at least dress himself, but he was always repeating jokes he'd read online and claiming he came up with them himself. Evan Bellman never said anything at all; he just sat there with the same bored expression.

Each time, Mikayla would suffer the accusations of her friends, saying, "You just don't know him," (which was often true) before finding the evidence against her current beau insurmountable. Then she'd say she had no idea what she was thinking and thank her friends for their good sense. The next week, about another boy, she'd say, "I just think he's cute."

So the cycle went. Suzanne had some crushes of her own, but those were kept under wraps, locked away in a place so private she could barely admit them, even to herself. It was a defense mechanism, she thought. And besides, she didn't really know these boys, just their names and faces and what they were like in a classroom. But what did they do outside of Perry Hall High School? Who were they when no teachers were watching?

She didn't know and she made no real efforts to find out. While this tactic precluded her from every getting to know any of them, it also saved her the embarrassment of finding out they were, ultimately, just high school boys. Treating them like filler NPCs turned them into filler NPCs for her.

But apparently Leo hoped he would see her again. She was already filing it away as a nice complement when Brit, who had been waiting since they left the Pyxian camp, just came out and said, "I want you to tell me you didn't program yourself a boyfriend."

"What?" Suzanne said, laughing half in surprise.

A wicked grin lit up Brit. "It makes sense. This game gives out a ton of experience."

Suzanne rolled her eyes. "Shut up. I told you I didn't program any of the NPCs. The game's AI built them all."

They walked on for a few more minutes before Brit spoke up again. "He seems like a nice guy is what I'm saying. He certainly knows how to handle his stave."

Suzanne scrambled for a comeback but couldn't come up with anything. Then Mikayla said, "Are you jealous, Brit?"

Brit laughed. "He's not really my type."

Mikayla shrugged. "He's probably the hottest NPC we've met so far."

"Have you been rating them?" Brit asked.

Mikayla ignored her. "How would hooking up even work?" she asked. Soon they found themselves speculating about what type of equipment the NPCs might have and what sort of skills would be transferrable into that kind of encounter.

Suzanne flushed. She wasn't going to tell Brit and Mikayla everything about Io. "I don't know," she lied. "It's not like any of the monsters we've killed have had anything dangling between their legs."

"Yeah, I was really dying to see a Hobgoblin's dick," Mikayla said. All three of them laughed. Suzanne found herself remembering how pleasant Leo's laugh was.

They had a few more skirmishes with monsters as they traveled south. Suzanne was surprised to find gargantulas on this side of the Ion River. When she'd programmed the game, she had meant for them to be monsters the players encountered only at lower levels. The girls were all approaching level twelve at this point, strong enough that giant spiders were more annoying than frightening. They didn't even have good loot drops.

"I swear," Brit said, "if I find one more loot drop full of anti-venom I'm going to kill every single gargantula in Io."

Suzanne plunged her dagger into the red eye of a gargantula. She watched her total experience go up by a measly two points as the monster exploded into pixels. In its place was a loot drop filled with more anti-venom. Suzanne tossed the anti-venom to Brit, who dropped it, rather than adding it to her inventory. "By the way, what's up with all these spiders? I thought they only spawned in Altair."

"It might have something to do with that." Brit and Suzanne looked and saw Mikayla pointing to the south.

Like Leo had said, the grassland suddenly dropped off into a valley. Scattered foothills broke up the landscape, each dotted with ruins. On the smaller hills there were collapsed cottages, and whole villages lay devastated on the larger summits.

In the distance, Suzanne could just make out what looked like the retaining wall of a larger city.

It was a fraction of Zenith City's size, but the sun shone on all of Pyxis, not just the Capital.

But Suzanne couldn't see as far as Mikayla could, and as they headed toward Pyxia, the city on the hill, she understood what Mikayla meant. Fluttering in the breeze, hanging from every still-standing building, was the flag of Altair. Four pillars supporting an orb, emblazoned in bloody red.

"The game set up the gargantulas to appear in Altair, right? Well, it looks like this is Altair now, too."

Mikayla stared up at the banner. The girls were standing outside what must have once been the city gates. Now they couldn't keep out anything. They had been collapsed, like most of the city and the castle.

A conspicuous silence and emptiness filled the area. In the real world, Suzanne thought, there would be bodies everywhere. It would all be a testament to the cruelty of the mad King Ramses.

But there were no bodies. There were no merchants in the squares, no guards in their stations. Just silence, emptiness.

"Fuck," Brit growled. "Now how are we going to get home?"

Suzanne was so absorbed by the emptiness, the complete lacking, that it took her a second to realize what Brit meant. Without a castle, there was no Oracle Chamber, no hack point. And without a hack point, they still didn't have a way to log out. They had come all the way to Pyxia just so they could disconnect from the game and return to reality. Now the reality of the situation was hitting Suzanne like a ton of bricks.

"Shit," she said, her voice so soft it didn't carry from her lips to the ears of her friends. "Shit, shit, shit." The word grew louder as she repeated it, echoing off the ruins of Pyxia.

That night they camped in the ruins of the Capital. Brit gathered the wood. She took two logs out of her inventory, combining the items to build a fire. That was how to a start a fire in Io. The flames maintained a pleasant amount of heat, never billowing smoke, as long as they were regularly fed more wood.

It was a simple enough task that neither Suzanne nor Mikayla had to help. They sat around the fire, watching the animated flames dance in their preordained shapes. Suzanne fidgeted with a stone, looking for some way to occupy herself. Aside from the crackling fire, there was only the silence.

Suzanne was finding it hard to think. Once again Io had proven to be a world capable of absolute bullshit. This wasn't what she had intended at all.

She couldn't help feeling partially responsible. Like she had failed as a game designer. She wrote the code that generated the personality of every single NPC and somehow that had made warmongers like Ramses. Had she failed to program basic morality into the NPCs?

She thought about the villagers in Oppold, who seemed to genuinely care about each other. That had to count for something. And the villagers of Reinke had helped her heal and move Brit.

But they were only repaying favors, a voice within her argued. You made them so they would repay debts. That's not morality, that's just good business sense. You scratch my back, I scratch yours. That's cold logic even a program can understand.

It was too much. Suzanne hurled the stone off into the night. It clattered off a broken tower, ricocheting into darkness. Mikayla put down her sword, which she was examining, and looked Suzanne in the eye.

"You can fix it," she said. "Once we're back home, you can undo all of this."

Brit stopped poking wood into the fire and looked up.

"That's right. All we have to do is get home."

Suzanne managed a smile, but the bigger question still nagged at her. The only remaining hack point was back in Ramses's castle, back in Altair. How on Io were they going to get home now?

# Chapter 7

In the morning nothing seemed better.

Suzanne lingered in her tent for as long as she could stand staring at the bland tarp walls. When she stepped outside, the ruins of Pyxia leered down at her. She wanted nothing more than to finish the destruction the Altair army had started. Well, that wasn't quite true. She wanted nothing more than to go home, but since that option was off the table, she wanted to break things.

She picked up a piece of rubble. Had it been part of a battlement? The cornerstone of some garden dais? Whatever it was, its item description now read, RUBBLE. And it was the right size for throwing. She hurled it at the wall. The rubble shattered into satisfying pixels.

The past few days had been so crazy she hadn't had much time to think about home. First they had escaped, then there was the whole thing with Brit, then Pyxis, and then Leo had . . . distracted her. She took the Pyxian hack point for granted, assuming that as long as they made it to Pyxia everything would be fine. Well, it clearly wasn't.

She walked around their little campsite, skirting the remains of the fire. Brit and Mikayla were still asleep in their tents. *At least I'm not alone*, she thought. She felt a surge of gratitude for her friends, for having two people she could count on in a world of crazy NPCs.

In the light of day, the ruins of Pyxia had their own charm. Ivy and weeds sprouted from the marble rubble, adding a touch of green to a field of white. The world was still quiet. Suzanne guessed the nearby monsters were nocturnal or had learned to stay clear of the former Capitol. Some would appear in the castle, now that the girls were here and the walls were broken. *It might be a good idea,* Suzanne thought, *to move before they show up.*

Then she heard footsteps. Soft footsteps, like soles of velvet. Yet they broke the silence.

Suzanne sat upright and they stopped. So she was being watched. Someone was trying to get the drop on her, and they knew she had heard them.

She huddled her cloak around her shoulders, trying to conceal her arms. They were behind her, she was sure of it. No need to show them that she was drawing her blades. No need for them to know she was ready.

First, she woke Mikayla. Mikayla immediately caught the drift. No doubt she heard the others as soon as she woke up. Her hand was at the hilt of her sword. Suzanne walked over to Brit and shook her awake.

Brit woke with a grunt and a snore. "Wha?" she said. The weak morning lit her face. "Gimme another hour," she said. "It's really hard getting comfy on a pile of rocks."

She rolled over, trying to nestle back into a comfortable position. Suzanne kicked her. "There's someone else here," she said. "Time to hit things."

"Oh good," Brit replied, rousing. She pushed herself up and withdrew her halberd from her inventory.

"Listen up, assholes," she shouted. "My name is Brit and I did not sleep well last night. My parents say I have anger issues. I'd like to work them out with your faces."

Her words echoed off the seemingly empty ruins.

"What the hell!" Mikayla hissed. "Now they know we know they're here!"

Suzanne still couldn't see who *they* were. But she knew she had heard footsteps. The girls were in the middle of what had once been a plaza, which meant there were plenty of buildings to hide behind.

"Let's start moving," Mikayla said. "We don't want to let them surround us."

"Do you know where they are?" Brit asked.

"At least one is behind that shop over there." Mikayla pointed at what had once been a merchant's, but was now little more than a façade.

"Good enough," Brit said. She raised her halberd and charged at the edifice.

There was a blur of motion and Brit threw herself down. Three throwing knives flashed past where her head had just been.

"Above you!" Mikayla shouted. An NPC seemed to fall out of the sky, swinging a one-handed axe down at Brit. Brit rolled to the side. The axe cleaved through the earth, leaving a long gouge.

The NPC wasn't as large as Brit, but his sleeveless robe showed off burly arms. He had short brown hair and a narrow face covered in stubble. A grey crown twirled over his head, but as Suzanne watched, it turned red. Suzanne recognized him as an Adept, one of the advanced Monk classes that specialized in Energite attacks. But he didn't seem to think Energite was necessary for dealing with Brit.

The Adept kicked at Brit's face. Brit blocked the kick with her forearm and pushed back. He stumbled, regaining his balance just in time to parry Brit's first swing. Brit's momentum carried her forward and now she stumbled. The NPC raised the axe again, but had to duck a dagger Suzanne threw.

Suzanne and Mikayla charged the NPC, who sprang backwards and shouted, "Now!"

Nine more NPCs sprang forward. From the looks of things, they were all in advanced classes.

"You are outnumbered," the Adept said. He spoke evenly and his face betrayed no emotion.

*Great*, Suzanne thought, *we're fighting a bunch of Pyxians.*

"You scared?" Brit asked, taunting.

None of the NPCs looked remotely scared.

"You will not last," the Adept said. He didn't

sound like he was making a threat, just observing the fact like one might say, "It's raining outside."

"Energite?" Mikayla murmured.

Suzanne nodded. She threw both the daggers she was holding at the NPCs. The Adept caught one with his left hand, and the other whizzed by a Paladin's head. But Suzanne hadn't been counting on them connecting. She just needed a moment to ready the Naphtha Bomb.

The attack pulsed in her hands, orange and red and bright white. Suzanne launched it at the ground in front of the NPCs. It connected with a crack and a boom, launching shrapnel in every direction. The NPCs threw up their arms to cover their faces. The Paladin closest to the impact was launched backwards into a wall.

"Run!" Suzanne shouted.

The girls dashed away, past the moldering gate into what had once been the courtyard of the castle. Vaulting over ruins, ducking under collapsed archways, they ran as fast as they could, but already the Pyxians were recovering and giving chase.

"They're gaining!" Mikayla yelled, and then she yelped in pain as a stone connected with the back of her head, sending her stumbling into a wall.

Suzanne saw her friend fall and sprinted over to help her up. Another rock flew at them, but Brit deflected it with the head of her halberd. Behind them there was a wall too high to climb over. In front, the Pyxian NPCs were advancing.

One of them twirled a sling with a sizable chunk of rubble in it. "You think," the NPC said, her voice sharp, "that you can reduce our homes to nothing and get away with it?" She was a Ranger, also wearing Pyxian robes and a sizable smirk.

She whipped the rock at the girls. It bounced off Brit's halberd with a high, ringing note.

"Calm yourself, Collette," the Adept said. Then, addressing the girls, he said, "You are surrounded, soldiers of Altair. If you continue to fight we shall be forced to kill you."

"Not that we'd mind," Collette sniped. But a look from the Adept silenced her.

"We're not from Altair," Suzanne said.

"No?" the Adept replied. "Then why is it you wear their armor and wield their weapons?"

"We got our shit in Altair," Brit snapped. "But we're not from there. We aren't part of their army! We don't want to destroy Pyxis, and we're not trying to fight any of you!"

"Then why did you attack Alphonse?" Collette replied, gesturing to the Adept.

"Because you were sneaking up on us like a bunch of fucking Assassins!" Brit shouted. "What, you think we were just going to wait for you all to surround us?"

Alphonse and Collette exchanged looks. If Suzanne had to guess, she'd say that those two were the leaders of the party. Alphonse whispered something in Collette's ear that sounded to Suzanne like, "Can't let them go," and dark lines spread across Collette's face.

"Absolutely not!" she said, her voice breaking too loud for a whisper. "They're too dangerous to take to Vale! What if they've been sent here to kill her? We'd be taking them right to her."

"We're not trying to kill anyone!" Suzanne shouted. "We just want to get home."

Alphonse cocked his head and stared at them. "Pyxia was your home?" he asked.

"No . . ." Brit began. She stopped, unsure of how to explain more.

Suzanne stepped in. "We come from a third kingdom," she explained. "And we heard that there was a room in the castle that could perform miracles. We hoped that the room would be able to take us home, but . . . " She gestured to the collapsed castle.

"What do you know of the Queen's Vault?" Alphonse asked. His voice, Suzanne noticed, was no longer flat. It was tinged with suspicion.

"Nothing!" Brit shouted. "We're not part of

some conspiracy! We don't know shit about any-thing! We just want to get home, okay?"

Alphonse considered her words for a second, his brow breaking into creased lines. He whispered some more words to Collette. Suzanne wished she had Mikayla's hearing, so she could listen to what they were saying. But Mikayla still looked pretty roughed up from her fall. What would they do if it came to a fight? They couldn't beat these Pyxians in a fair fight, and Suzanne still had two minutes left to recharge her Naphtha Bomb.

After what felt like an hour, but was really less than a minute, Alphonse turned back toward the girls.

"We are going to take you prisoner." Brit began to protest, but he talked louder over her. "Please understand it is for our own safety. If you are Altairi, we cannot let you go. We are going to take you to meet our leader, in Vale. If she deems you to be allies, then we will release you from your bonds. Otherwise we will have to dispose of you here."

"You really want to fight?" Brit asked.

"We do not," Alphonse replied. "But the question is, do you?"

# Chapter 8

Hands bound, the girls followed Alphonse and his companions out of the city. The Pyxians kept the girls separated as they marched. Suzanne could have freed her hands at any point, but what would that accomplish? She'd never get away, and the Pyxians would have even less reason to trust her if she tried to make a break for it.

Where they were marching she didn't know, but they left the city on the hill and headed west with the sun at their backs. Once more the countryside of Pyxia sprawled before them. But where before it had all been open grassland, there were now frequent outcroppings of stone. The grass was low and coarse. Soon they were marching uphill again, toward the mountains. Suzanne wanted to ask Alphonse where exactly this Vale place was, but he might assume she was gathering intel for Ramses.

The stones that broke from the earth glittered with fantastic minerals. Even the monsters that appeared, squadrons of gnome Warriors riding dire pumas, were flecked with the variegated colors of the realm.

As prisoners, the girls didn't do any battling. Watching the Pyxians fight, Suzanne thought that she would only be in their way. Collette, Alphonse, and the others fought with the same efficiency as Lynx and Leo.

Collette and another Pyxian peppered the creatures with projectiles, while Alphonse ran in and dealt out massive melee damage. The other NPCs used midrange weapons to finish off the weakened monsters before they could even attack. The strategy decimated small clusters of monsters with ease.

Suzanne wondered how NPCs had learned to play the game so efficiently. It was like watching Lynx and Leo all over again. They didn't fight like NPCs, but like serious gamers with the experience of a childhood filled with RPGs.

After a battle with a particularly dedicated group of mountain Satyrs, the company broke to rest and tend to their wounds. There had been more Satyrs than first imagined; one had managed to land a nasty bite on Collette's wrist.

"It's fine," she said, jerking it away from a old Monk named Mallon, who had withdrawn healing herbs from her inventory. The monsters in Pyxia dropped herbs as loot instead of potions.

"They can chew through swords, those Satyrs. You're lucky I got him off before he took your hand with him," Mallon said.

Of all the Pyxians, Mallon seemed to be by far the oldest. Her face was creased with wrinkles and her braided hair was dull gray, the same color as the stones she rested up against. Mallon seemed to be in charge of guarding Suzanne, never straying too far from her.

Evidently her age counted for something, because when she made a second effort to tend to Collette's wounds, she didn't get any more back-talk.

Once Mallon was done, Collette flexed her shoulder. "Thank you," she sniffed. She shot Suzanne a dirty look before stalking off to find Alphonse and plan for the rest of the day. Mallon saw Suzanne watching and winked.

Once she was sure Collette was out of earshot, Suzanne asked, "Is she always like that?"

Mallon chuckled. "Only since she was born. I'm hoping tomorrow's the day she'll lighten up."

The old NPC walked over to Suzanne and sat down beside her.

"So tell me. Are you lot really spies and assassins sent to kill Queen Libra?"

"No!" Suzanne said, ready to defend her reputation. Mallon merely laughed.

"Alright, alright, simmer down. Just fooling with you. And for the record, I don't agree with my daughter. If you were a bunch of killers, I can't figure what you'd stand from letting yourself get captured like this. You'd fight for the glory of Ramses, whatever that's worth."

"Collette's your daughter?" Suzanne asked.

"Course she is," Mallon replied. "Where d'you think she got her looks from?"

"You two just seem so . . . " Suzanne paused, trying to come up with words that wouldn't offend.

"Different? Sure. But if you live long enough, you run out of energy for being angry all the time."

Now that she knew Mallon and Collette were mother and daughter, Suzanne studied the older NPC more closely. In Altair, the girls had met an NPC named Hawthorne who cared for his two grandchildren, but she'd never met a mother and daughter.

Mallon hadn't gone through a pregnancy—
Suzanne knew that. The AI algorithm had
assigned Mallon a daughter and then a baby Collette appeared, aging at the regular Io time. Both
Mallon and Collette had grey crown icons instead
of grey diamonds. Suzanne wondered if that was
hereditary.

Now they were really hiking. Suzanne realized they were going to march straight into the
mountains. But the mountains of Io were not
the mountains of Earth. They weren't formed by
tectonic shifts but by the imagination of a sixteen-
year-old girl.

Picture a mountain and a mountain range.
Little more than glorified triangles, right? Each
mountain rises until its peak, where it then tumbles
down into a valley only to rise into the next peak.
Of course, this is an oversimplification, but as a
guiding principle of design it works well enough.
It's how children draw mountains: a bunch of triangles, overlapping in the distance.

But in Io, there was no need for such formal constraints, which was why Suzanne abandoned the mold while designing the mountains of Io.

When they came to the first mountain in Pyxia, Mikayla stopped and gaped. "It's going to fall," she said. "There's no way it can stay up."

The mountain rose, like mountains do. But it was less a triangle and more an upside-down parabola. The stone sprang from the earth, arcing over a couple of hills. It curved back down to the earth. It looked like an archway, something manmade, but on a scale so massive that it was, in the world of Io, irrefutably a natural phenomenon.

Suzanne, staring at the Looping Mountain, felt pride fill her body. This was cooler than she had ever imagined while plugging away at her computer.

Contrary to what Mikayla expected, the mountain stayed up. They camped for the night in the shadow of the spectacular mountain. The Pyxians let the girls set up tents. Alphonse took watch while the others slept.

The next morning they marched onwards, the landscape growing more fantastic. Natural bridges, barely wider than a character, spanned huge chasms in the earth. Giant slabs of shale balanced precariously by the rugged path. If you brushed into the mountain facades they would crack and collapse, splintering into hundreds of small stones.

The robes of the Pyxians began to make more sense to Suzanne as well. The hard terrain required the party to be flexible, and her armor hampered her movement. Still, she was only wearing the hardened leather of a Rogue. Brit, trapped in her Fighter's armor, could barely swing her legs over the rock faces. The fact that their hands were still bound didn't make things any easier.

Brit bumbled into one of the shale mountains. The rock fell back, cracking into pixels with a loud crash. When the mountain path was quiet again, Collette heaved a fake sigh that was unpleasantly reminiscent of Gretchen, Suzanne's least favorite person in the real world.

"Are we going to have to carry her?" Collette said.

"That will slow us down," Alphonse replied.

Collette laughed but Alphonse looked serious.

"Just untie them already," Mallon argued. "We'll be climbing soon, and they'll need their hands then."

# Chapter 9

Up, up they went. Suzanne's health bar was chipped away from scrapes and bruises. She had never been rock climbing in the real world, not even on a plastic wall in a gym. Scaling a mountain without any equipment was something she had never dreamed of. Her player character was way more athletic than she'd ever been, but she wasn't confident she could make the climb in-game either.

The red rock of the mountain was merciless. The girls were gradually passed by all ten Pyxians as they climbed, until they brought up the rear of the line. *On the mountain,* Suzanne thought, *we aren't even a threat.*

"It's like they're spiders," Brit panted. Suzanne nodded, not wanting to waste her breath on words.

"Whatever you do," Mikayla groaned, "don't look down." The ground was a dizzying distance beneath them, their own grips the only thing holding them to the mountain. At least they'd have time to reflect on their lives if they fell.

"It's like we're climbing all the way up to Zenith City," Brit said.

Suzanne did her best to follow the Pyxians' path. They were all experienced climbers and knew which handholds were the best and which ledges could support their weight.

But in some places they were too experienced for the girls to follow them. Alphonse grabbed a handhold and swung his legs like a pendulum. His momentum carried him sideways over the mountain face, depositing him on a secure ledge.

"No way," Brit said, as the other Pyxians

followed his example. Mallon was the last to swing across, but she made it fine. The NPCs stared at the girls expectantly.

"We won't make it," Mikayla shouted across.

Alphonse shrugged. "It's the only way. I'm sure you'll be fine."

Suzanne managed a weak laugh. "I think he meant that to be encouraging," she muttered. Brit and Mikayla nodded. Mikayla, Suzanne noticed, looked a little sick.

Suzanne scooted past them. She reached out for the handhold but it was too far away. She stuck out her arm as far as she could, but the only way to grab that far would be to step off the ledge she was balanced on, and there was no way she was trying that.

"Jump for it!" Collette suggested. She clearly enjoyed watching the girls struggle. Suzanne fantasized about pushing Collette off the ledge once she made it across, but she wasn't sure if she'd be making it across at all.

"Brit," Suzanne said. "Hold onto my hand. Make sure I don't fall and die, okay?"

Brit nodded. With her right hand she clutched a handhold and with her left she grabbed Suzanne's wrist.

When Suzanne first tested Io with the TII, she had fallen to her death a few times. That was before she put permanent death in. Weirdly enough, the game never let her experience impact. She got the GAME OVER message and was kicked back to reality before she hit the ground. But now there was permanent death . . . Suzanne made sure she didn't look down as she leaned forward and took her first step off the ledge.

Reflexively her left foot scrambled for a foothold, but there was none. She told herself to lean into the fall. It didn't help that her heart was pounding in her chest. But she leaned further away from the ledge and felt the handhold with her fingertips.

"Just a little farther!" she shouted. Brit sidled across the ledge to give her more slack. Suzanne grabbed again and her fingers found the groove in the rock. She lifted her right foot off the ledge and swung out, her right hand flailing upwards to find her left.

As she swung like a pendulum, Suzanne realized how little control she had. Unable to resist, she looked down and saw only the mountain, an unyielding rock face that she would bounce off, smashing into countless ledges and jagged outcroppings if she lost her grip. And she could feel her hands beginning to slip . . .

Then Suzanne felt a hand grab her ankle. She saw that Mallon was holding her foot, pulling her onto the ledge with the Pyxians. They made space for Suzanne to walk to a wide part of the ledge, so she could rest and try to calm her heart that was thundering in her chest.

Mikayla went next. Her player character was taller than Suzanne, so she could reach the handhold without stepping off the ledge. Instead of swinging across, she bent her body double and walked her away between the two ledges. Mallon grabbed her too and helped her onto the other ledge. Suzanne hugged her hard and together they turned to watch Brit.

Brit grabbed confidently for the handhold. She began to swing across, her body dangling from the tiny groove. There was a faint snap as the handhold broke clean away. Brit fell backwards into nothing.

For a second everything was still. Suzanne saw Brit fall, saw the horrified look on Mikayla's face. She ran forward, pushing past the Pyxians and throwing herself down after Brit.

"Grab me!" she shouted as they fell. Brit wrapped her arms around Suzanne's waist as Suzanne drew her daggers.

"Backstab!" she shouted, activating the special attack. The blades glowed white with the energy. Backstab scored critical hits when you struck an unsuspecting enemy. Suzanne hoped it would work on a mountain. She slammed her daggers into the rock face, the blades cutting through the stone like a knife through butter.

Now they were sliding down the mountain, their feet scrabbling for some foothold. But then the special attack and the blades lost their glow. They ground to a halt, Suzanne belly-flopping into the mountain face.

"Shit," Brit whispered. Suzanne agreed with the sentiment. Her arms would've ripped out of their sockets in the real world.

"Are you okay?" Mikayla shouted down from above.

"We're totally fine!" Brit yelled back. "Take your time!"

Suzanne looked up and saw Mallon running down the side of the mountain. She was moving so fast her silver hair streamed behind her, two whips coiled around her waist like belts. When she was halfway between the ledge and where the girls hung, she turned around and lashed a whip up toward the Pyxians. Alphonse caught the line and secured it by wrapping it around his body.

Mallon kept descending until the line was tight. Then she dropped another whip down to Suzanne and Brit.

"Brit first," she said. Brit grabbed the line and began to pull herself upwards, hand over hand, back to the ledge. Mikayla grabbed her hands and pulled her up onto the ledge and into a hug.

Once Brit was safe, Mallon shouted, "Whenever you're ready, Alph." To Suzanne, she said, "You might want to hold on."

Alphonse muttered some words to himself, activating a special attack. He wrapped the whip around his hand one more time and pulled with all his might. The line jerked upwards with such force that Suzanne could barely hang on. She flew upwards, past the ledge, and fell back down into Brit's arms.

"Thanks," Suzanne said, breaking out into relieved laughter.

Brit laughed too. "Any time. Actually, no, fuck that. Let's never do that again."

"Try not to," Mikayla said. She was stone serious.

"If you're ready then," Alphonse said. "We can keep going."

"What the shit, dude?" Brit said, putting Suzanne down. "I almost just died! Give us a second to be happy I'm not dead, okay?"

Alphonse offered a thin smile. "I'm grateful you did not fall. Besides, we're done with the climbing. It is only half a day's walk to Vale from here."

Suzanne couldn't see how that was possible. The ledge was barely wide enough for them all to stand on. It didn't lead around the mountain or connect up with another ledge.

Alphonse saw her looking confused. "What good is a secret hideout if anyone can find the way in?" he asked.

He walked past Suzanne and knocked three times on the rock face. "It's Alphonse," he said.

A dot of light appeared in the mountainside. It extended vertically, making a line. Then both ends of the line extended horizontally, then vertically again, tracing the outline of a rectangular door in the stone. The rectangle faded away into nothing, revealing a dark passageway straight into the mountain.

The girls' hands were bound again, but not as tightly as before. Alphonse explained that it was a necessary precaution they had to take whenever someone came to Vale for the first time.

Alphonse took the first step into the mountain and beckoned the rest to follow him. Mallon took the rear, with Suzanne, Brit, and Mikayla walking right in front of her. They were barely a few steps into the passage when the portal out of the mountain ground shut, sealing them inside.

The passage was almost completely dark. In the real world, Suzanne's eyes would have adjusted eventually, but she trudged through the mountain in perpetual, unyielding darkness. She could see her health bar and the rest of her display, but she couldn't even make out Brit's head in front of her. Still, even though she couldn't see, her other senses still worked.

She felt her way through the passage, her hand never leaving the left wall. The wall was rough, like it had been hewn out of stone using tools. Wherever they were headed, it was downhill. Great, she thought, that means we'll have to climb all the way back up if we ever want to find our way out of here.

The only sound in the passageway was the scraping and shuffling of the party's footsteps over the stone corridor. Suzanne lost track of how long they had been marching. Eventually the ground began to level out. Soon after that a light appeared at the end of the tunnel, no bigger than a pinpoint at first, but widening as they approached it.

Suzanne's eyes were so used to the darkness that she had to shield them as she stumbled toward the exit. As she took her first step out of the tunnel, she closed her eyes against the glare. Instead of the hard stone, her foot sank into soft, loamy earth. And unless she was hallucinating, the air around her was filled with birdsong.

"Looks like you finally made it, Alphonse," Suzanne heard a voice say.

"Yes, milord," Alphonse replied.

"No need to stand on such courtesy," the voice replied. "I'm glad you're all safe."

"As I am glad for you. Is your sister here in Vale?"

"They both are. You're to report to Libra once you've recovered from your journey."

Suzanne knew that voice. She looked up from the ground. Her eyes still hadn't adjusted, and the edges of things were cast in a blurred halo. Through squinted eyes she saw Leo, framed in light and looking absolutely shocked at seeing her.

# Chapter 10

"What are you doing here?" Leo asked. Suzanne wanted to ask him the same question. A thin, golden circlet held up his hair and he was dressed in robes of flowing purple. It was a far cry from the plain, traveling gear he was wearing when she'd seen him last.

Suzanne stared at him. It wasn't just the clothes. His whole aura had changed.

"We're taking them to be questioned," Collette said.

"Questioned? Why?"

"Those were our orders," Alphonse replied.

"The queen sent us to find these foreigners and bring them to Vale."

"How did the queen know they were here?" Leo asked, confused. "I never told her about Suzanne or any of the others. And besides, these are my friends. There's no need to question them."

"The queen disagrees," Alphonse said, politely, but just as firmly. "Even if they are not from Altair, as they claim, they are not Pyxians. We must be careful, my prince."

"You're a prince?" Suzanne asked. Leo and the other Pyxians stared at her, like they had forgotten the girls were there. Leo broke into an embarrassed grin.

"Well, yes," he said sheepishly.

"And you didn't think to mention that?" Mikayla asked, her voice incredulous.

"Obviously, he didn't want to reveal his true identity to the likes of you," Collette sneered.

She winced as Mallon smacked her on the head. "Mind your manners, child," Mallon said. Then, turning to Leo, she added, "Since you're familiar with our guests here, you might as well be the one to take them to your sister. They ought to see her before Alphonse makes his report. No need to keep these girls tied up longer than necessary."

"Our report can wait, milord," Alphonse said.

Leo bowed slightly to Alphonse. "Thank you, elder Mallon, I will. Please, follow me." Leo's voice took on a note of respect Suzanne had never heard before when he addressed Mallon.

"Then we're off," Mallon said. With Collette and Alphonse, she strolled into the grassy median field which separated their current location—the slopes above the city—from the city proper. Higher up on the slopes was another jagged mountain climb.

Suzanne was dying to ask Leo questions about being a prince, but he seemed determined to talk about anything else. After he ignored three of her questions she resolved to corner him later. For now she had to accept his tour-guiding.

"We're inside the mountain," Leo explained,

leading the bound girls off toward the north part of the city. "It was a volcano a long time ago, but it stopped erupting. This all grew up on top of volcanic rock," he said, gesturing at the lush greenery.

There were no streets in Vale, only narrow alleys between buildings, overgrown with bristling mountain grass. None of the buildings had doors. Instead, curtains hung over empty frames. Almost all the curtains were drawn as NPCs chatted with their neighbors. Like in the tent camp, the Pyxians waved to Leo as he passed and he stopped frequently to say hello.

They passed in front of the barracks, shaped like an overlarge inn, where most of the NPCs slept. "This was where the Pyxian army was stationed, in older times," Leo said. "We moved the government here after the Altairi invasion."

Turning right at the barracks, they saw an armory and an apothecary, along with a few tents for generic merchants and a hexagonal building with a domed roof, which reminded Suzanne of a mosque.

The mosque-like building surprised Suzanne. It was the only decorated building they had seen so far in Vale. Most of the structures were cut from the same volcanic stone, ranging in color from charcoal to jet-black. The domed building was made of a white stone like marble and its dome was a cool shade of turquoise. It towered over every other structure in Vale.

"What is that place?" she asked Leo.

"That's the Oratorium," he replied, as if that explained everything. "Now, come on," he said, "we must not keep the queen waiting."

Leo continued past the Oratorium, winding his way through more narrow alleys. The long shadows and black buildings made Vale a confusing town to walk through. Every corner looked the same until Suzanne realized she could orient herself by the Oratorium on the horizon. Every time she used the domed building to reorient herself, she wondered what function it could possibly serve.

They passed another armory before Leo came to a halt in front of a small house. Compared to the barracks and especially the Oratorium, the house looked like nothing, more like a cottage in a village than the dwelling of a queen. It was the same black stone as everything else. But Leo signaled it was their destination and ushered the girls inside.

To be fair, the house was larger on the inside than it looked from the outside due to the weird dynamics of house-building in Io. Still, it was about the size of the apartment she shared with her dad back in the real world, and that place was hardly fit for a queen.

The house was a single room simply furnished with a table and chairs. In the corner was a low bed with a short nightstand. There were no lamps or other light sources, but the porous volcanic rock let in enough light to illuminate the room. The walls were dotted with countless holes to let the sunlight in, which made the walls glow like they contained a fire within themselves. So despite the starkness of the room, it felt comfortably warm.

There were two NPCs in the room, one sitting and one standing. Suzanne immediately recognized the standing NPC as Lynx. Like Leo, she was dressed in far more elegant robes, and a thin circlet rested on her forehead. Lynx nodded to acknowledge Suzanne, but didn't offer anything beyond that.

The NPC sitting in the chair was undoubtedly the queen. She didn't have a crown as opulent as Ramses, but instead wore a simple circlet like her brother. Her golden hair tumbled all the way down to her lap. She wore a plain, charcoal robe; the same shade as her throne, although it was less a throne and more a chair.

Like her brother, she had a kind face, but behind her smile were two wary jade eyes. Libra looked from girl to girl, searching their faces. For all the world it reminded Suzanne of getting grilled by a teacher back at Perry Hall High.

"Sister," Leo said, placing his fist over his heart and bowing low to the woman sitting in the chair. Suzanne noticed how his voice changed when he addressed the queen. "These three foreigners are not our enemies. I have fought alongside them and I know that they deserve our trust and respect."

"If they are truly deserving of our trust, then why did you not tell me about them? When Lynx spoke of them, she did not call them enemies, but she said they were powerful enough to pose a potential threat. Do you disagree?"

Leo shook his head. "They are all capable fighters."

"You helped them enter Pyxis and guided them toward our capital. And yet you said nothing. Did you not consider the appearance of three strange, capable fighters worth reporting to your queen?"

Brit cleared her throat. "Um, hello," she said. "We're standing right here."

The queen turned toward Brit and smiled. "Yes, I am aware." Turning back to her brother, she said, "Thank you, Leo. You may go."

Leo bowed stiffly and walked out the door.

"And you as well, Lynx." Lynx hesitated, as if she didn't want to leave the queen alone with Suzanne and her friends, but she left as well. Once her siblings were gone, the queen turned toward the girls. "My name is Libra, queen of Pyxis. I would know your names."

Suzanne stepped forward. "My name is Suzanne. This is Brit and Mikayla. It is an honor to meet you."

"I see you are not from Pyxis," Libra said. "But you are not from Altair either."

"Your majesty," Mikayla began, but Libra raised a hand.

"Please, only the pompous, like my brother, stand on such formality." She broke into a wide smile. "You may call me Libra if I may address you by your names. May I?"

"Of course!" Mikayla said, a little too loudly. "What I was going to say, Libra, is that we come from another, secret kingdom. It's called Baltimore."

"Baltimore?" Libra asked. "And where is this Baltimore?"

"Across a sea, beyond the mountains to the east," Mikayla replied.

"We don't know how we came to this land," Suzanne ventured. "We, uh, were told by King Ramses of Altair that if we helped him dispose of a monster, he would use his Oracle Chamber to help us get home. But the king betrayed us, tried to have us killed, and when that failed, he threw us in prison."

Libra frowned. "We had a similar chamber in Pyxia," she said.

"Yeah!" Brit exclaimed. "That's why we came to Pyxis in the first place. Your brother and sister helped us across. Then we split off from them and headed to the Capital but it was wrecked. We were trying to plan our next move when Alphonse and Collette showed up and took us prisoner."

Libra remained silent, staring at them. "So, uh, that's our story," Brit added lamely.

"Indeed," Libra replied. "It's certainly an interesting one. If you were given the opportunity to return to Baltimore, would you?"

"Definitely," Mikayla said.

"Allow me to present another option," Libra said. "Stay here in Vale. Help us defend against Ramses. The three of you met the king, you served in his army, and fought his battles. You could tell us much about our enemies that we do not know."

"We'd be happy to help while we're here," Suzanne said, "but we've got to get going."

"Wait," Libra said. "Listen to what I have to say. If you help us, we will begin rebuilding the Queen's Vault. Once it is completed, you can use the chamber to return to Baltimore."

"There's got to be a catch," Brit said.

"No deceptions," Libra said. "However, the

rebuilding will take time, how much time, I cannot say. But know this—once Ramses's army is no longer a threat, we will put all of our effort into returning you three home."

*Can NPCs even make a hack point?* Suzanne wondered. *Can they fix the broken one?* But what was she doing? How was she even considering Libra's offer? The last thing they needed was to get tangled up with another batch of Io royalty. She didn't think Libra would ever reveal herself to be as screwy as Ramses, but they couldn't wait until a war ended to get home. They needed to leave Io as soon as possible.

She was about to tell Libra, *no*, when Brit spoke up, and said, "Sure."

"I don't know about Suze and Mikayla," Brit continued. "But I really wanna fuck that Ramses guy up, you know? I want to make him pay for all this bullshit." She smiled at her friends apologetically. "I know you want to go home. I do, too, but if we mess Ramses up on the way that'd be even better. Besides, I wouldn't be standing here if it wasn't for Leo. So if this pays him back, even better."

Suzanne couldn't believe what she was hearing. Then again, Brit had risked her health to defend a random village, so random acts of bravery weren't out of the ordinary for her.

"They might not even be able to rebuild the Queen's Vault! Our best bet is still the Oracle Chamber," Suzanne argued. "Come on, Mikayla, tell her that she's being dumb."

Mikayla frowned. "Sorry," she said, "but I agree with Brit. We need to at least straighten our heads out and come up with a plan. And I'd rather do that here, where we won't have to keep looking over our shoulder for Ramses's soldiers. I think it makes sense to stay here."

"You guys . . ." Suzanne began, but she didn't know what to say. She could tell that Brit and Mikayla had made up their minds. They thought

Libra was the better bet for getting home. That was too much for Suzanne.

"Excuse me," she said, her voice trembling. Suzanne turned and walked out of Libra's house, ignoring the voices of her friends calling her name behind her.

# Chapter 11

It was Leo who found her.

Suzanne wandered through the alleys of Vale without much thought to where she was going. Her brain was occupied with untangling what had just happened. Was she really upset with her friends? She didn't know. Her mind was spinning its wheels but going nowhere. She couldn't understand why she had gotten so upset and that upset her all the more.

She heard Brit calling her name and ducked into an alleyway, out of sight. Her friends were the last characters she wanted to see right now.

Pressing on, she took a left and a right,

walking further and further away from Libra's home. Suzanne looked down at the grass in the alley. Each square foot was identical, copy-pasted to form the terrain of the alley.

She couldn't just ignore that. She couldn't ignore the obvious flaws in everything, and she didn't understand how Brit and Mikayla could. She looked up at the dome of the Oratorium and tried to focus on its color—the way it caught the virtual sunlight—and tried to forget that it was virtual sunlight. But the world of Io felt so small to her.

Unbidden, memories of other games came to mind. Not the ones she had finished, the ones she had loved, but the ones she had abandoned after a week of playing. Some had lagging combat systems or buggy menus or the graphics that looked like crayon drawings. Whatever reason, they'd end up back in their boxes, to be sold for a pittance in store credit at a game shop.

They all shared one common thread: they all

failed to immerse her. They failed to silence the concerns of a world outside themselves. The games she abandoned were eminently pausable. She didn't care if her save files got deleted. These were the games where she only ever invested time, never emotions into playing them.

Games could be an escape from how shitty real life was. That's what she had been feeling when she logged into Io on that Friday night. There was reality, which was filled with disappointment, with parents who died and grew distant and bullies at school and the stifling mediocrity demanded of her by pretty much everyone, and then there were games, which demanded she be the best. By their own limited rules, games demanded she excel. They accepted nothing less.

But in Io, the games had become her reality. There was no escaping, no way to do something else. And if that was how the game was going to be, then fine. Suzanne would play it until she won, which she thought meant that finding a way out mattered more than anything else. Brit and Mikayla clearly didn't feel the same way.

Suzanne walked into a cluster of merchant tents. She walked up to one and pretended to take an interest in one of the many Pyxian robes. The Merchant stared at her with scrutiny. It might have been because of her Altairi garb, but nevertheless it made Suzanne feel uncomfortable and she slipped away without buying anything.

She heard Mikayla calling her name from another one of the streets, but didn't respond. She still didn't want to see her friends. She looked to the left and the right to make sure no one was watching her and made a quick dash toward the Oratorium.

Inside, the building was cold. Altitude didn't translate to temperature in Io like it did in the real world, so the temperature in Vale was no colder than it had been at the foot of the mountain. But inside the Oratorium, it was so cool that she half-expected to see her own breath. Of course, she hadn't programmed that in, so it didn't happen.

But it was cold, the coldest she'd been in Io. She shivered, grabbing a dire puma pelt from inside her inventory and equipping. Instantly, she began to feel warmer. The fur was soft to her touch.

Like Libra's house, there were no lights inside the Oratorium. But from the inside the dome was revealed to be translucent, filling the single hexagonal room with pale blue light.

The inside of the Oratorium was like a museum. Each floor above the first had a square hole in the middle, where you could look down to the floor beneath. Spiral staircases connected each floor to the next.

Statues occupied most of the floor space in the Oratorium. All the statues were of NPCs, labeled by their class and their name. Former kings and queens of Pyxis stood next to Citizens. The statues were carved of volcanic rock. They caught the blue light of the room in their pores, glowing like the sky after dawn.

She looked from a grim-faced king to a Swordswoman mid-thrust. Some of the statues wielded weapons, but just as many captured their subjects reclining. An Assassin whittled a tree branch and a Sniper's peerless gaze was turned on a scroll.

The faces of the armed statues showed every range of emotions Suzanne herself had experienced in battle: elation at victory, pain in defeat, and beyond all else, absolute concentration. Suzanne knew what it was like to ignore everything else and focus completely on a battle, and she saw that reflected in the narrowed brows and furious gazes of several statues.

The other statues, though, beamed and frowned and grimaced for countless other reasons. The whittler was biting her lip in concentration. A statue of a Berserker, carrying what looked suspiciously like a barrel of ale, offered a bleary-eyed smile. A Swiftblade, one of the advanced Ranger classes, laughed with crinkled eyes.

Some of the statues were joined together. A Fighter held hands with a Ranger, a Troubadour whispered into a Paladin's ear. Suzanne found herself gravitating toward the non-combative statues. She wandered among them, her hand occasionally reaching out to touch an especially lifelike feature.

Not lifelike. She had to remind herself. The statues and those depicted in them were not alive. They were characters in a game.

Yet in the presence of so many faces her resolve began to weaken. Each of the statues suggested a story, a character whose life was lived with richness she could only imagine. They themselves might not have been human but their expressions certainly were.

Suzanne thought back to her first lonely days in Perry Hall High School. That was what it was like in the Oratorium: she was surrounded by a history she felt like she would never learn. She bumbled through the hallways, doing her best to stay out of the way. She'd catch snatches of conversation: the end of discussions about boys, complaints about teachers, and speculation into the social lives of others. Never enough to get the whole story, but enough to suggest there was one.

Just like these statues. Perhaps the Fighter and the Ranger were lovers. Maybe the Sniper spent more time sharpening her quill than sharpening her arrows. These characters were more than their classes or a health bar to be exhausted.

She was so engrossed in her thoughts that she didn't hear the footsteps of someone else entering the Oratorium.

"I thought you might be in here," Leo said.

She turned to see Leo silhouetted in the entrance. He began walking toward her, weaving his way through the rows of statues. Suzanne lost sight of his slender body as he stepped behind a statute of a Dragoon, but then he reappeared just a few steps away from her. When she first saw him in Vale, he seemed surprised, and in the presence of the queen he seemed nervous. But now he seemed at ease, more like how he was on the Pyxian plains, despite the princely clothing he had equipped.

"What is this place?" she asked.

"It's the Oratorium," he responded deadpan.

She rolled her eyes and turned back to the statue. She was hardly in the mood for a dose of Leo's levity.

"It is a memorial." This time his voice was much softer. When she turned to look at him again, his face was more somber to match his tone. "Our bodies disappear when we die."

Suzanne knew that. Characters, like everything else, became pixels when their health was reduced to zero. She had designed the game that way so loot would be easier to collect. But now that she thought about it, it seemed a little callous on her part.

"Well, it's rotten," he said. "It leaves nothing for those left behind."

She realized he wasn't speaking in generalizations, but from his own experience. "You have your memories," she suggested, but as soon as she said it, she regretted it. It sounded like the same kind of vague bullshit guidance counselors told Suzanne after her mom died. Just because it was true didn't mean it was helpful.

Leo nodded half-heartedly. "But sometimes it helps for there to be something a little more tangible. So they made the Oratorium, a place to speak for those who can no longer speak for themselves. And it's a place for us to speak whatever sorrow is on our hearts."

He walked past her to the statue of the laughing Swiftblade. "This is my mother," he said. "She was poisoned and we could not heal her. I could not heal her."

He stared at his hands before continuing. "Sometimes I think, this *was* my mother. But this is who she is, to me, to all of us, forever. She is laughing, happy."

Suzanne wondered what her own mother would look like as a statue. She had a gravestone, just etched rock on a plot of grass, but that seemed infinitely less personal than the memorials in the Oratorium.

As much as she hated to admit it, sometimes when Suzanne thought about her mom all she could picture was the gravestone. Suzanne still had other sensory memories of her mother—Suzanne could still hear her mother's voice singing the multiplication tables, and she could still feel the gentleness of her mother's touch as her mother washed Suzanne's hair. Those impressions had not faded. *But,* Suzanne was too afraid to think, *what if they do?*

Suzanne realized Leo was looking right at her. "I'm sorry, I must not make much sense."

"No, of course it does," she said. She didn't know what else to say so she put her arms around him and hugged him. He stiffened before embracing her in return.

"It's awesome," she whispered. She hoped he knew she meant it.

He pulled away and smiled. "So what happened with my sister? I heard Brit shouting your name. She kind of explained."

Suzanne frowned and said nothing.

Leo laughed softly. "You're lucky Libra didn't take offense. Of course, nothing does seem to offend my sister, but still . . . "

She stared into his inquiring eyes, wondering how she could begin to explain the thoughts running through her mind. It wasn't like she could say she was tired of living in a video game. Then she remembered what Burgrave had told her about how the Pyxians believed they all had a strong purpose. Maybe in those terms he could understand.

"I feel like I should be trying to get home," she said. "Like more than anything else, that's what I should be doing."

"I see," he said, trying his best not to look disappointed.

She leaned against the statue of the drunk Berserker. "But I don't want to leave this place without helping. I want to help you and the rest of the Pyxians. I want to put Ramses in his place, but every minute I do that is a minute I'm not trying to get home. So I feel guilty, because no matter what I do, I feel like I'm letting someone down. Like I'm abandoning someone."

"You must have people you love at home," he said.

"I do. My dad's got to be missing me by now."

Leo didn't ask about her mother. It was like he already knew.

"Do you know how to get home?" he asked.

She shook her head. "It looks like our best bet is in Zenith City. But . . ."

"But nothing!" he cut in. "What you say makes perfect sense. But you cannot get home now. So why not fight with us? We will free our kingdom and then push the invaders back to their Capitol. We will make them suffer as they have made us."

His eyes blazed with anger as he spoke. She found she could not break eye contact. His anger seemed to enliven him, making his words sound more urgent, more vital. She'd never felt this kind of anger. After her mom had died . . . it hadn't been anger. Sure, there'd been moments when the injustice overwhelmed, episodes of angry grief that she remembered in snatches. But most of mourning for Suzanne was like she'd shut down.

"Then, once we have righted Ramses's wrongs, we will go back to Zenith City. We will march to his castle and throw him from his throne. And you can pry open the door to his secrets and use whatever you find to find your way home."

His voice softened but his features didn't. Leo's anger sharpened him, refining him into someone she couldn't quite decide whether or not she liked. And this uncertainty about him legitimized the entire world to her. His depth was Io's. His anger was more than a character trait, it was an emotion he felt as much as she felt confused or lost or afraid.

And she felt very much afraid. It wasn't the claustrophobic fear that she felt in the Lamia's caves, or the plunging terror when Brit fell while mountain climbing. He was staring at her like they were the only ones in the world.

Her throat didn't feel dry. She didn't hear bells ringing in her ears and her stomach's contents, while unknown, certainly did not contain butter- flies. The rules of Io maintained that the sensation of her body stay constant. But her mind was firing on all cylinders, countless thoughts—*Do I want this?*—*I don't even know him!*—*He's an NPC!*— raced by too quick for her to fully consider. She felt like a bystander in her own life. She felt—laughing internally as she realized—like she was watching a cutscene in a game.

He leaned toward her, mouth saying nothing, eyes implying everything.

Suzanne shut her eyes.

The curtain was pulled back as feet slapped on the stone floor. Collette ran into the Oratorium.

Leo and Suzanne performed an awkward shimmy away from each other.

"You've got to come now!" she shouted. "There are monsters on the mountain!"

# Chapter 12

As Suzanne ran out of the Oratorium after Collette, she heard the sound. Faint at first, but then louder. A thrumming noise, an ominous noise. Her instinct was to duck, like with a low-flying airplane.

It was getting closer, each thrum timed like a drumbeat. And then she saw—not a drumbeat, but a wing beat. Hundreds of winged monsters beat their wings in unison, flying up and over the lip of the caldera.

They wheeled around in the sky overhead, out of range of arrows and other projectiles, but close enough for their piercing cries to echo throughout

Vale. They were like nothing Suzanne had ever seen—in Io, at least. The monsters looked just like gryphons, but Suzanne hadn't finished programming the gryphons into the game yet. They shouldn't have been in Io at all.

That hardly mattered when half-lion, half-eagle monsters filled the sky.

Panic spread rapidly among the Citizens of Vale. Merchants ran for the safety of their shops. Older NPCs grabbed children off the street and ushered them into shelter. They thought they were safe with the mountain walls to protect them. But Vale, the impregnable stronghold of Pyxis, had been breached.

"I need to find Libra!" Leo shouted. Suzanne watched him disappear down an alley, wondering where Brit and Mikayla were.

The gryphons' cry pierced the air. The monsters dropped to earth like rain near the rim of the caldera.

"Come on!" Collette shouted, running toward

the outskirts of the city. Suzanne followed after her. She wondered if there were enough soldiers in Vale to hold off all the monsters. But then another ear-shattering cry split the air and a second wave of gryphons appeared in the sky.

Cursing, Suzanne followed Collette's winding path through the narrow streets of Vale. They met up with Alphonse, Mallon, and the rest of Collette's group in the field outside the city, but there was still no sign of Brit and Mikayla.

"What are these things?" Collette asked.

No one else in the group seemed to know.

"They're gryphons," Suzanne offered. The NPCs stared at her dumbfounded. "Flying monsters. They've, uh, got really sharp claws."

"How would you know a thing like that?" Collette asked, her eyes narrowed in suspicion.

"They're common where I come from," Suzanne lied.

"We've got bigger problems," Alphonse muttered. "Look."

He pointed up the cliffs where the monsters had landed. From this distance Suzanne could just make out soldiers dismounting from the gryphons. It wasn't just a swarm of monsters. The gryphons were the steeds for an invasion.

More and more Pyxian soldiers were finding their way to the field. Lynx appeared with a group of Snipers. She acknowledged Suzanne with a nod while other Ranger characters bolstered her ranks. She led them off to take a position closer to the invaders.

Suzanne kept waiting for someone to appear and start issuing orders, but the Pyxians moved into position. They prepared for this, she realized. She dared to feel a little hope.

Lynx's ranged unit started firing in volleys, trying to keep the gryphons and their riders pinned to the mountainside. The invaders had to climb back up to avoid the projectiles. But they had the advantage of height which let them shoot farther. Soon they were firing their own arrows down at the Pyxians from a distance that the Pyxians couldn't return fire.

The Pyxians dragged out every bit of cover they could find. Chairs, tables, and doors were taken from houses and set up as a barricade. Suzanne joined the rest of the defenders in crouching behind the shelter, listening to the arrows from above bouncing off the volcanic rock.

"We're the ones who're pinned down now," Alphonse grumbled. He and the rest of the melee units were frustrated and useless in a long-range fight.

And that was becoming a major problem for the defense. The invaders split into two groups. One continued the projectile pressure, while the other made its way down into the valley of Vale.

Lynx and her Snipers were doing their best to hold off the assault, but they had to risk leaving cover in order to get a shot off. Already one of her Snipers had taken a critical hit from an invader's crossbow. The Pyxian pixelated as the rest of the defenders watched.

Suzanne crouched behind a table with Alphonse, Collette, and Mallon. Collette jumped up, whirling a stone from her sling. Immediately, she flung herself down under cover as an arrow whizzed by where her head had been.

"One down," she said, a broad smile on her face.

Alphonse didn't share her optimism. "We won't last," he said. "We always figured if someone got into Vale they'd be attacking from the tunnels. We never thought anyone would come up over the rim."

His voice had taken on the flat, frank tone of a Pyxian in a crisis. Mallon nodded, calm as her countryman. "And what's to stop them sending off those flying beasts for another batch of soldiers? Fact is, we don't know how many more of them there are. But as for us, we've only got the soldiers we have now."

"You've got us," Brit shouted. She and Mikayla ran in a crouch out from the city streets.

"And we've got a plan," Mikayla added. "Well, Libra has a plan. But she sent us here to tell you the plan, and also, you four are going to be doing it with us."

"Where is the queen?" Alphonse asked.

"She's coming with Leo out to the lines. They're going to try to draw the invaders' attention away from us."

"But will they be okay?" Suzanne asked, thinking about Leo.

Mallon chuckled. "I don't know how they make them in Baltimore," she said, "but in Pyxis our queens can take care of themselves."

The rest of the Pyxians laughed. Clearly Libra was not an NPC to take lightly.

There was a crackling sound and then an arrow burst through the barricade. "They're using Energite!" Alphonse hissed.

"We've got to move, like, yesterday," Brit said.

With her leading the way, they dashed back to the shelter of the city streets. Once within the protection of Vale's buildings, she stopped, looking at the tangle of alleys.

"Hey Al, you know how to get to the barracks from here?" she asked, a little sheepishly. Wordlessly he took the lead. Suzanne found herself running just to keep up with the rest of the group. As they sprinted through Vale, Brit sketched out the finer points of Libra's plan.

Before they split up to enact the plan, Suzanne pulled Mikayla and Brit aside for a second to talk about the gryphons.

"What do you mean they shouldn't be here?" Brit demanded. "Then why are they here?"

"I'm telling you I don't know," Suzanne replied. "It's like the Lamia all over again."

That was going to have to be enough for Brit.

Suzanne really didn't know how the gryphons were in the game.

"Did you manage to get a good look at them?" she asked Mikayla.

"No, they were too high up. How do we fight these things? Are they like normal monsters?"

Suzanne shrugged. "No clue."

"Well, fuck," Brit said. "You could've mentioned this before we climbed up here to fight them."

They went their separate ways for the plan. Now Suzanne was perched on the rim of the caldera. The stone here was weak, ready to break away without any notice. Suzanne could see both Vale and the country around the volcano at a nauseating distance below. She forced herself to look up and focus on her target, an outcropping of stone above the invaders.

That was Libra's plan. Start an avalanche to crush the enemy. She showed Brit a secret route up to the top of the mountain, which was how Suzanne had gotten up so high.

Suzanne didn't know if the plan would work. What if Shadow Walk didn't work on these monsters? What if the avalanche failed? But it was too late to back out now. She had to press forward and hope for the best.

On the other side of the rim, Mallon was swinging her way into position. She was even higher up on the mountainside than Suzanne, but it was necessary because she couldn't go into Stealth Mode. The plan relied on Brit and Alphonse's diversion to get Mallon into place.

The footholds around the rim were narrow and Suzanne had to check where she was putting her foot down before each step. She needed to go faster—at this rate Mallon's charge would go off before hers. She wobbled to maintain her balance on the unstable footing, but she didn't fall. And below she saw the diversion kicking off.

Lower down, where the footing was more stable and there was more space to maneuver, Brit and Alphonse ran toward the invaders. Brit had her halberd out and she was swinging it overhead. Alphonse bashed his twin axes together. Both of them were shouting—Suzanne could just make out one of Brit's scathing "fuckheads" from her distance.

The diversion appeared to be working. The invaders' ranged units kept firing down on the Pyxian defenses while their melee units along with a dozen gryphons headed downhill toward Brit and Alphonse. The first gryphon flew in too close and Brit swatted it out of the air with her halberd. But just because it was grounded, the beast was no less dangerous. And now more were flying down to join the fight.

Suzanne tore herself away; she had to trust the others. She had her own job to do, and it was almost her time. Mallon had covered enough distance that she was no longer swinging but crawling along the top of the mountainside. She hardly need have bothered: all of the invaders not firing down on the Pyxians were watching the skirmish with Brit and Alphonse.

Suzanne was fifty yards away from her position—a small outcropping that extended like a diving board over the heads of the invaders—when two things happened. First, she saw that two of the invaders were posted like sentries right by where she needed to be. They looked like Rangers and were carrying long spears. On their breastplates was the four-pillared insignia of Ramses.

Her footing came loose. Suzanne stumbled, slipping and tumbling a few feet downhill, breaking her Shadow Walk.

Both of the sentries snapped to attention. Suzanne stayed where she had caught herself, hoping they'd think it was just some rocks breaking loose. She was half-buried by some stones that followed her down. Maybe they wouldn't see her.

But she remembered this was Io. Rocks didn't break loose here unless you made them.

The sentries were climbing down toward her, too close for another Shadow Walk to work. She needed to move or they'd have the advantage. With their spears, they could easily keep her pinned down defending herself.

Suzanne waited until one of them was level with her. She sprang up to standing and hurled a rock at the Ranger's face. He lifted up his spear to block the rock, but that left him defenseless against Suzanne tackling him. They grappled for a few steps before the Ranger pushed her off. Suzanne gave him a two-handed shove in the chest. His arms flailed out as he fell backwards into the empty space, tumbling head over heels before landing with a sickening crunch far down the mountainside.

She didn't have time to watch his fall. The other Ranger stabbed at her head and she threw herself down flat to dodge. He was on a much wider ledge than she was, allowing him more space to launch his attacks. He was so fast with his spear that she didn't have time to equip her daggers. She could only duck, unable to backpedal out of range. He drove her back until she was at the edge of the ledge.

Out of room to maneuver, she had to make her move. He thrust his spear with two hands and she stepped forward to catch the shaft, the spearhead nicking her cheek. She turned and threw all her weight into his motion, pulling him off balance, off his ledge. But the only place he had to fall was right on her and together they tumbled into a freefall.

But now she was free to equip her daggers. "Backstab!" she shouted, slamming her blades into the rock face. And as before they sunk into the stone, stopping her fall. Her body slammed into the mountainside but she held onto the daggers. She heard the impact of the second Ranger and began to pull herself, hand over hand, back up to outcropping.

Perched atop it, she waited for the signal from Collette, and she watched Brit and Alphonse fend off the invaders as best they could. They kept moving, making it hard for the invaders to surround them. Alphonse lashed out with his two axes, hacking through enemies. But they weren't falling to his blows. These were trained soldiers, as ready to take damage as they were to receive it. Suzanne lost sight of Brit and Alphonse in the crush of bodies.

A blazing projectile flew through the sky: the signal from Collette. Suzanne deposited the last of her Energite in a Naphtha Bomb and set it right below the outcropping. She retreated a safe distance along the rim and watched the rest of the plan unfold.

Mallon's charge went off first, sending a stream of debris tumbling downhill. Then Suzanne's bomb exploded and the two cascades of stone joined. They battered downhill, prying loose other rocks and turning into a bona fide landslide.

The gryphons were the first to notice something was wrong. Those highest up were crushed in a roar of stone but further down the mountain they took flight. The invaders saw their mounts taking flight and turned just in time to watch the earth bury them alive.

Down, down the avalanche went, picking up steam and growing in size. By now the invaders had time to react, and they split wide, running from the torrent of stone. But there were too many of them and not enough footing. Those in the middle failed to make it out in time. The avalanche collapsed some of the ledges they had perched on, sending more of them falling to their fate.

Brit and Alphonse were still fighting off invaders. "Get out of there!" Suzanne shouted, but her voice was lost in the landslide's roar. Brit grabbed one of the Altairi by the ankle and used him to batter invaders out of the way. Alphonse turned away from the fight, readying some kind of Energite attack.

Brit tossed the limp invader into a group of his fellows and reequipped her halberd. Launching herself in the air, she brought her weapon down in a massive slam. Even at the mouth of the caldera, Suzanne could see the crack Brit made in the ground.

The invaders had jumped to the side to avoid Brit's attack, and now they finally seemed aware of the landslide charging toward them. They hesitated, some wanting to keep the fight going, but a larger group was running for cover.

Alphonse stepped forward, straddling the crack in the ground. His axe-blades glowed with Energite. His voice broke clearly over the cacophony: "Terraform!"

He chopped diagonally upwards with both blades, slicing into the earth. But instead of breaking free, the axe-blades pulled the earth up after them. Terraforming was one of the special abilities Suzanne designed for Adepts, but she had no idea it would be so effective. A stone wall rose, guided by his right hand, and another by his left. They came together to form a barrier, like the point of an arrow.

Brit ran forward and through her bulk behind the barriers, reinforcing them. And they held. The landslide split around the point of the arrow, diverting toward where the invaders were trying to find shelter. Stones plummeted downhill, battering into and breaking through the makeshift barricade the Pyxians had erected. But they had already retreated into the safety of Vale.

The rumbling and the roaring reached a crescendo and then it was over. The silence after such a cacophony was narcotic. Suzanne stared down at the altered landscape. She could see survivors trying to regroup. Some marshalled back in a semblance of a formation, while others tried desperately to free their buried comrades.

Suzanne saw a large bolder launch up into the air. Out of the hole left in its wake crawled Brit, followed by Alphonse. His barriers had held. They made their way down toward Vale, Brit supporting Alphonse as he limped along.

The avalanche lurched, and for a second, Suzanne thought more earth might fall. But it was that the dying had died. Their bodies exploded into pixels, collapsing the structures they supported. The rocks settled quickly into new formations. Infinite pixels blew upwards from the landslide. They shimmered upwards, twirling toward the sky. It was like someone had taken all the stars from the night and thrown them into the air. Suzanne stood mesmerized—she had never seen death on this scale. It was beautiful and awful at once.

Mallon swung over to her. "Come now," she said. "We're going to be needed down below in a minute. We've got to get back to the others."

Suzanne nodded but didn't move. The pixels rose up in the air, past where she was perched. She felt Mallon's hand on her shoulder. "It won't do much good thinking twice now," the old NPC said. "What's done is done. If they had half the sense you do, they wouldn't have come here in the first place."

Suzanne let Mallon lead her back toward the path down to the barracks. They made their way slowly down, checking each hand and foothold in case the avalanche shook it loose. Once they were at the bottom, Suzanne looked back up at the sky. The pixels were still not finished with their dance.

# Chapter 13

"It's not over," Leo said. "They're regrouping." He had the same blazing look in his eyes as when he had spoken in the Oratorium. "They're regrouping and they'll be marching on us by nightfall. We've got to act now and wipe them out."

Suzanne watched him shift his gaze through everyone in the room, daring them to challenge him.

"Your boyfriend's a little crazy," Brit said.

"He's not my boyfriend," Suzanne whispered back. Brit sounded like she approved of Leo's plan, which only made Suzanne less sure of it.

Leo was speaking in the main room of Vale's barracks. Libra and Lynx were there, as were Alphonse, Mallon, and Collette. The rest of the room was filled with other classed NPCs Suzanne didn't recognize, as well as Merchants and other Citizens.

One of the Merchants spoke up. She was a middle-aged NPC, dressed in flowing Pyxian robes. "While I applaud Leo's fervor," she said in her ponderous voice, "I can't help but notice that his plan would leave Vale undefended. If, say, further reinforcements were to join up with these invaders, then who would defend the city from assault?"

Her words met with murmurs of support from the Citizens present. At once, Suzanne understood why Libra had insisted on inviting Citizens to the meeting. All of Vale, not just the warriors, was under attack. So all of Vale would have a voice.

But not everyone valued that voice the same. "If we strike now, we won't have to worry about defending Vale. There won't be anyone left to defend it from!" Leo was nearly at the point of shouting.

"Hannah's point is valid," Libra said, nodding to the middle-aged NPC. As the queen spoke, the murmuring in the room disappeared. "Our enemies have surprised us once already today. We must not allow them a second chance."

She rose from her seat and walked to the center of the room. "That means we must seize the initiative. But not blindly," she added, glancing at Leo. "We do not know how many of our enemies survived the avalanche."

"Can't we just call them what they are: Altairi scum?" someone called out. Other NPCs nodded and murmured their agreement.

Libra waited until the voices fell silent. "We are at war with King Ramses of Altair, yes. And he fights his war with his army. But that does not mean we are at war with the Altairi people, nor does it mean that they are, as you have so eloquently put it, 'scum.'"

"That's right!" Lynx chimed in. "If we were judging people by their rulers, than you'd all be as ugly as my brother!"

Laughter filled the room. "So we will attack," Libra said. "But before we march on our enemies, I want all of you to help move everyone toward the center of town. And I expect volunteers to lead the city's defense while we lay our enemies to their final rest."

With her words, the meeting was adjourned. Suzanne made to leave, but Mikayla caught her arm. Libra was motioning for the three of them to come over by her.

"I want to thank you for what you did," she said. "It saddens me that such a measure was necessary. And it saddens me that I must ask you to accompany me on the front lines, but I must."

"We weren't gonna ask to stay behind," Brit replied. Suzanne nodded. Why was Libra making such a big deal out of this?

"There are some in Vale," the queen said, "who

do not trust you three fully. And while I disagree with them, perhaps during an invasion is not the best time to entrust the defense of my people to three foreigners."

Brit laughed. "We'll just have to save their asses to change their minds."

Libra smiled. "I am grateful you understand," she said. "Please, equip your armor and fight by my side. I would have three such as you in my retinue while making war."

Suzanne held her daggers in her hand. It was funny how used to their weight she had become. Like a controller, she thought, smiling within herself at the comparison. As far back as she could remember she was gaming. Her real hands nearly had calluses from gripping controllers. Certainly she had thicker skin on her fingertips from PC gaming.

She looked down at the hand that was not her hand. She'd reached this level of coordination with games. How many hours had she spent over-shooting platforms in *Portal* before she mastered the platform genre? Now those games were hardly an effort for her.

She was getting that good with her daggers. They weren't the first pair she'd owned in Io, but thanks to her design, all the daggers she'd owned had weighed the same. She was more than coordinated with these weapons, she realized. Her body had fluency to it that only her fingers had previously achieved.

She looked to her left, to Brit weighing a new halberd. Brit's previous weapon was lost in the avalanche. The new one was larger, but not as comically big as Brit would've liked. Still, Suzanne could tell her friend was delighted with the new weapon.

She looked to her right, to Mikayla, who stared straight ahead. Her sword was slung over her shoulder and her guard was strapped tight to her wrist. Whatever she was feeling, she looked absolutely ready for battle.

Day turned to dusk as the sun dipped below the peak of the mountain. The sky was enflamed in red. From somewhere behind her, Suzanne could hear the NPCs of Vale barricading themselves in the center of their city. She did not look back.

Before her, Libra stood at the head of the assembled troops. Suzanne expected another speech, but the queen merely nodded and stepped into the ranks. Then, as one, they began their march on the remnants of the invaders.

Over the new terrain they went, the empty graves of gryphons and invaders crushed in the landslide. Ahead, Suzanne could see the army of the enemy gathering. She glanced at their health bars; most had a chunk missing. Good, she thought, we need every edge we can get. Even with their forces devastated by an avalanche, they outnumbered the Pyxians two to one.

From the mass of enemies a Paladin stepped forward. "Enemies of Ramses!" he shouted, "Throw down your weapons and your lives will be spared."

Libra stepped ahead of the rest of the Pyxians. "I will not look down on any who take him up on his offer. Although I do doubt the sincerity of his words."

No one made to leave.

"Why don't you throw down your weapons?" Brit yelled up at the Altairi. "You'd save us the effort of walking all the way up there and taking them from you."

"You know not who you insult!" the Paladin shouted back. "I bring the justice of the king of Altair! You have one last chance to surrender before we mete out his judgment."

"Take your king's judgment," Brit replied, "and shove it where the sun don't shine."

"For Ramses!" the Paladin shouted. The other Altairi took up the cry. The army surged downhill toward Vale.

"Lances forward!" Libra shouted. All the Pyxians with poled weapons stepped forward. Lynx raised her naginata and Brit thrust the axe-head of her halberd forward. The Altairi's momentum carried them right into the wall of blades the Pyxians held out for them.

Their front line decimated, the Altairi troops fell back and regrouped. Their second approach was much more cautious. The Pyxians fell into defensive ranks and the two forces met in earnest.

It wasn't like any other encounter Suzanne had been in. Fighting monsters in a forest or bandits in a town was one thing. This battle was something else entirely. Suzanne was used to a finite number of enemies, being able to outmaneuver and over-power her enemies. But in the battle on the hill there were too many Altairi to just outthink them. No, she sunk her dagger into the stomach of a Fighter and immediately threw herself to the side to dodge a cleaving sword.

She looked up and saw the Paladin crier. He

lopped at Suzanne's head. She tried to parry with a dagger but the strength of his blow forced her to sidestep off balance. Seeing an opening, the Paladin thrust his sword forward. Suzanne had to throw herself down to get under his blade.

But the Paladin swung his sword up and made to drive the blade down in her stomach. She threw one of her daggers into the gap between his helmet and his breastplate. She rolled back on her shoulders and sprung to standing with a kick, knocking the Paladin over and landing on his chest. She pulled out her dagger as his body faded to nothing.

Yet she couldn't relax. Everywhere she looked there were more Altairi. She fell back beside Brit, who had just relieved an Altairi neck of its head.

"This is going to stop being fun in a minute," Brit muttered.

Suze glanced at her health bar. Still two-thirds full, but against so many enemies, it wasn't clear how long that would last.

"Where's Mikayla?" Suzanne said, slinging a

dagger at the face of an Altairi Fencer who fell, clutching her eye.

"I think she's over by Libra," Brit replied. "Let's go find them!"

She lowered her shoulder and charged into the tangle of battle. Suzanne followed in her wake, slashing at the Altairi who had the good sense to get out of Brit's way. From somewhere nearby she heard Collette's sling whirling and thwacking into an enemy's head.

Brit stopped abruptly and Suzanne ran right into her. Peering around her friend she saw why Brit had stopped: there was a giant Berserker in the way.

His fists were encased in iron spheres the size of beach balls, studded with spikes as long as a Suzanne's middle finger. "Come on then," he shouted, smashing the spheres together. The clang reverberated through the air. "Let's see what you got!"

Brit swung her halberd at his neck. The Berserker

lifted a hand and lazily deflected the attack. It was hard to tell because his helmet covered his face, but it sounded like the Berserker was laughing.

"You go low, I'll go high," Suzanne said.

Brit charged forward, raising her halberd. But at the last moment she stopped and spun, swinging her halberd low at his legs. Suzanne ran toward the two of them, launching herself off Brit's back, planting both her daggers up to their hilts in the Berserker's shoulders. Brit hacked out his legs and the giant NPC fell.

"Not bad," a voice said. Suzanne spun around to see Libra standing there. The queen's war attire was barely different from her regalia at court. Her hair was pinned up behind her head and she wore a thicker robe. Her only weapons were a pair of ornate knuckledusters covering her hands and a pair of spurs attached to her heels.

The queen smiled. "But here comes another one. Allow me to handle it."

As she said, another mace-fisted Berserker was

charging toward them. He swung a fist at the queen's head. She punched the iron sphere and it shattered, falling to pieces on the ground. The Berserker roared and swung his other fist, but Libra merely stepped aside. Then, grabbing his arm, she used his momentum to slam him on to the ground. She stood over the fallen Berserker and administered a crushing blow to the Altairi's face. The blow pixelated the Berserker, and Libra's momentum carried her fist forward into the earth.

The queen flashed Brit and Suzanne a smile and threw herself at another enemy. They kept on searching for Mikayla, finding her crossing swords with an enemy Ranger. She wasn't in any trouble. Mikayla's sword was a flash of silver, weaving around her opponent's guard. With a thrust and a twist, the other Ranger found himself without a weapon; another slash left him without any health.

"They just keep coming," Mikayla said. "It's like *Gears of War* on hardcore survival mode. Enemies keep spawning and you keep killing them and they keep spawning until you die."

"We're gonna kill all of them," Brit said. "I didn't realize . . . I guess that's how we end it."

"Yeah," Suzanne agreed. There seemed little else worth saying. Every single one of them. After an hour of battling her mind was exhausted, but her character's body was still running hot. The girls stuck together in a loose unit, dropping back to an outcropping to heal up whenever one of their health bars got too low. Most of the fighting was concentrated where the hill broke into a plateau. From their rock they had a good vantage point, but even while they were resting they had to be on guard.

The sun was fully set, flickering torchlight taking its place. And still the battle raged on, the two sides crashing into each other, retreating, reforming, and charging in again.

Collette led a group to reinforce the Pyxians' right flank. She swung her loaded slings like they were flails, smashing down any Altairi who challenged her. Suzanne could hear Collette barking orders to the rest of their crew, shouting for them to hold the line.

But the flank was collapsing under the Altairi's numbers. Pyxian reinforcements were mired in the crowded battlefield. The Altairi reinforcements, riding on the gryphons, had no such problem. A flock of screeching beasts descended on Collette, momentarily blocking her from view.

Suzanne heard a roar of anger as Alphonse came hurtling into the fray. His twin axes cleaved through the creatures, severing wings from bodies and heads from necks. But he couldn't fight his way through the Altairi horde. Meanwhile, Collette's party began to drop, one by one, beneath the claws and blades of the Altairi forces.

She took a step toward the throng of Altairi, but Brit grabbed her and pulled her back.

"There are too many of them!" she shouted. "You'd never get there in time."

Suzanne saw Alphonse jump high above the enemy, crashing back down to the ground. He used his Terraform attack to drive a rift in their forces, but the Altairi came crashing through. Suzanne saw a volley of Altairi arrows fly toward Alphonse and Collette, she saw Collette shove Alphonse to the ground and . . . Suzanne looked away. Brit was right—there was nothing that she could do, not anymore. Collette's pixels drifted high above the battle, where no one could hurt her anymore.

And yet, no matter how grim things looked, there was Libra and her younger siblings, holding the center of the Pyxian line nearly by themselves. No one could get close to the queen. Her four limbs lashed out and struck down any Altairi foolish enough to try. Behind her, Lynx and Leo performed their synchronized, wheeling attack, dealing with the Altairi who chose to run around the queen rather than joining their comrades in the dirt.

At one point, Suzanne looked up and saw the

pixels of the fallen rising upwards. They blended into the sky, adding countless stars to those already glittered. Then an Altairi Dragoon caught her in the chest with his maul, lifting her from the earth and sending her crashing backwards.

Her vision flickered; she felt her health bar dropping dangerously low. She saw Brit charging at the Dragoon. She rose to join back in, but an arrow hit her in the shoulder. Instantly, her eyes fell heavy and she crashed forward onto the ground. Mikayla ran over, shouting her name, and yet, before she closed her eyes, all Suzanne could think of was how there were too many stars, too many Altairi, too many, too many . . .

Suzanne drifted awake in a dark room. Leo stood over her, using his powers to Cleanse her.

"Thank you," Suzanne said weakly.

"You're okay," Leo said. Suzanne felt a wave of

exhaustion come over her and she drifted back to sleep.

She woke hours later in the same darkened building on the outskirts of Vale. For a second she thought the fighting might be over, but even from where she lay she could hear the sounds of conflict.

"It's nearly over," Mikayla said. Suzanne could barely make her out, her body silhouetted against the window.

"What happened to me?" Suzanne asked.

"Sleep arrow."

*That explains why Leo was healing me*, Suzanne thought. "Where's Brit?"

"She's outside, keeping an eye on things. We're supposed to head back out there once you're up."

Suzanne sat up and put her feet on the floor. "Okay."

"No," Mikayla said, stepping away from the window. "Not yet."

For a moment, she was silent. When she began

to speak, the words tumbled out of her mouth, one after another. "You know my parents don't let me game, right? That's why I'm always over at your place. They think games are all mindless violence, all hack-and-slash bullshit. They never listen to me, no matter how much I argue that they aren't all like that. But what we did tonight . . . they all had personalities. Even the filler NPCs have something to say. They have families."

She shook her head. "I guess what I'm trying to say is that the game is mindlessly violent. Because all this fighting is mindless. When we were out there I felt myself stepping away, zoning out of it, you know? If I think about it too much it makes me sick. All this killing, all this destroying, I don't want to do it anymore. But that's the way this world works."

She fell silent. The sounds of the battle were quieting as well. Suzanne took a deep breath and asked, "What are you saying?"

Even in the darkness Suzanne could tell Mikayla

was staring straight at her. "I don't know. Maybe nothing."

They waited until the sound of battle began to die. Then Suzanne put her feet on the floor. They stepped out into the night, ready to accept the spoils of such a victory.

# Chapter 14

There was no celebration after the battle. Suzanne, Brit, and Mikayla rejoined the fighting in time to watch the last Altairi fall. It was a Sniper. She fell with little ceremony: an arrow to the neck. A squad of Pyxians went out to collect loot. Everyone else went home to sleep.

After the fighting, Leo found them. He was still wearing the ruins of his princely attire. Suzanne didn't think he had healed since the battle ended. Still, he managed a smile for Suzanne.

"Can you wait up just a little longer?" he asked. "My sister, the queen, would like to speak with you three."

It had been a long night and it was only going to get longer. As she walked beside Leo, Suzanne shoved her daggers back into her inventory. She wasn't planning on taking them back out for a while. A few minutes later they were at Libra's door, facing the scrutiny of heavily armed guards. They hadn't been there the last time the girls were at Libra's, but that was before the battle.

The guards weren't the only difference. The mood inside Libra's was dour, almost like they hadn't won the battle at all. Libra herself was unusually taciturn, acknowledging the girls with a nod before resuming her whispered conversation with Alphonse. They took seats next to Mallon, who was stone-faced and silent. She had come back from the battle and her daughter had not. Suzanne couldn't begin to imagine what to say.

After a wait that seemed like an eternity, Libra cleared her throat and turned to address the gathering. "Our current strategy," she said, "is untenable. We can no longer remain passive in this war. Perhaps it was a mistake to stay inactive for so long."

Libra looked to Leo who sat by her right hand. A look of embarrassment appeared on his face, but Suzanne saw smugness mingled in his flush. She knew he'd wanted to fight back from the beginning, and that seemed to be what Libra was saying.

"We will leave Vale. I have already sent out emissaries to the other holdouts. We will marshal an army for Pyxis and retake our lands. The time for passivity has passed. It is time we engage Ramses on his terms. It is time we make war."

She paused, yet no one dared speak. "I look at the faces of those gathered here," Libra continued, "and none are joyful. This gives me hope. Though we must pollute our lands with combat, we will not pollute our hearts. We will strike as necessary until the Altairi learn the error of following a king such as Ramses."

Again she fell silent and again no one challenged the silence. Suzanne studied Libra's face.

As always, it was composed in a neutral expression. But Suzanne could feel the sadness that suffused her words, leaking through her mask of composure.

"If anyone believes this is a foolish path to walk, speak now. We are about to move beyond the realms of doubting into a war of actions. Soon the time for dialogue will be behind us."

Leo muttered something. Suzanne, along with everyone else, turned to stare at him.

"What was that brother?" Libra asked.

"It's not enough," he said. "We might retake our lands from the Altairi, but as long as Ramses is their ruler they will be a threat to us. We must not stop at our own borders. We must dethrone that despot to guarantee our safety."

"Yes," Mallon said. She did not look up from the table, but kept staring at her hands clenched together. "Leo is right. This war will not end until we end it."

Murmurs of assent broke out around the table. Suzanne looked over at Mikayla, who shook her head. But she and Brit held their silence. Suzanne understood: it wasn't their decision or their war.

Mallon spoke again, her voice monotone. "When you encounter a monster in the wilderness, you don't push it back to its den. You put it down. You deal with it."

"We aren't conquerors," Lynx said.

"No one's talking about conquering," Leo retorted. "We're talking about ensuring peace."

"Funny how your talks of peace involve more war," Lynx spat back.

Libra banged her fist on the table. "Enough," she said to the startled company. "We will not squabble like children. I would know what our guests think."

She looked at Suzanne who stared back in amazement. *Why does she want our opinion?* Suzanne saw Brit and Mikayla were staring at her expectantly.

"I . . . " she began, but what could she say? Leo smiled at her encouragingly. Did he think she would agree with him? She didn't know what

Libra expected her to say or what was right. So she could only say what she felt.

"I think the war will be terrible," she said, her voice gaining strength with each word. "I don't think any of us really know what it would be like to fight in a war. But we," she paused, gesturing to Mikayla and Brit, "we have to head to Altair. It's our only way home. So if your army is headed there then we will fight beside you."

"And if we only seek to free Pyxis?" Libra asked. "If we drive the Altairi to the river and stop once they are on the other side?"

"Then we will be by your side until we reach the river," Mikayla answered. "We're going east anyway, and it's not like we're any less safe with your army than we'd be alone."

"And then you would cross into Altair to continue your quest?"

Brit laughed a syllable. "Yeah, we have to, right?"

Suzanne nodded. "It's not our war but if we're picking a side we're picking yours. But we can't stay here forever to help you keep the peace. So once we reach the Ion River, we're going to head toward Zenith City."

"But that's beside the point!" Leo burst out. "What the three of them do is not the question at hand. Will we take the necessary measure to protect ourselves?"

Libra shook her head, her eyes closed in a pained expression. "You forget, brother, that though we war against a nation led by Ramses, we battle with his subjects. They are no guiltier of starting this war than you or I. It is their fate as those born under the sway of a mad king."

"And yet," she continued before Leo could interrupt her, "your arguments are not without merit. But as Suzanne has said, this will be a long war. Perhaps we will find that the Altairi's support for Ramses crumbles by the time we have liberated our lands."

And with that, the meeting was dismissed. Suzanne was following Brit and Mikayla out of the room when she felt someone catch her arm. It was Leo.

"Could we talk privately?" he asked. He looked as haggard as the rest of the NPCs, but he was filled with a nervous energy. He couldn't seem to stop moving, shifting his weight from one foot to the other and fidgeting with the fringes of his robe.

"I'll be back in a sec," Suzanne said to Brit and Mikayla. Brit looked like she was about to burst out laughing.

Suzanne followed Leo to the alley beside Libra's house. Compared to the clamor of battle, the night was empty and silent. The moon was high over Vale, filling the tiny holes in the volcanic rock with countless winking specks of silver. Suzanne felt calm. She felt as still as the night.

"I'm glad you weren't harmed in the battle," he said. "And I'm glad you'll be with us in the campaign."

"Thanks. I'm glad you're okay, too."

"And I was wondering if you would . . . I mean,

if you'd be interested in . . . " he stammered, growing redder in the face.

Suzanne turned away so he wouldn't see her fighting back laughter.

"Look," she said, "I think you're cute, okay? We're going to be spending a lot of time together and we're both going to be under a ton of pressure. So maybe try to not to get so worked up over everything?"

She turned to face him. He blinked at her, dazed.

She had to stand on her tiptoes. She sprang forward and kissed him. And maybe it was because she was so tired, but it almost felt like his lips were really on her lips. Like they weren't in Io at all but at a drive-in movie, at a school dance, alone in the entire world.

"I've got to get back," she said, "but I'll see you around." She turned around so he wouldn't see her face flushed with embarrassment and excitement.

Suzanne found Brit and Mikayla loitering by the entrance to Libra's house.

"So?" Mikayla asked.

"So what do you want to do for the rest of today?" Suzanne asked, playing innocent.

Brit laughed. "Look at you! Too fucking cool. Did you leave him standing in that alley?"

Suzanne couldn't help herself; the giggles broke out of her.

"Suzanne!" Mikayla said, sounding scandalized. "He's a prince! You can't just go making out with princes and leaving them in alleys!"

They laughed all the way back to the barracks. Unconsciously, Suzanne touched her lips with her hand. Was it just her imagination or could she still feel her first kiss lingering?

# Epilogue

Somewhere on the walk their chatter gave way to introspection. By the time they reached the barracks, they were all silent, all engaged with their own thoughts.

Brit wanted to talk to her friends, she wanted to keep laughing. But she allowed the silence to reign as they went back into the barracks, past rows and rows of bunks stacked three high. All around, NPCs removed their armor and slid into bed, nodding off the instant their heads hit the pillow. Did they dream? Feel remorse? The girls couldn't know. The NPCs slept.

They passed into the officers' quarters—

sectioned-off rooms that allowed for some small amount of privacy. Still, Brit found herself unable to speak. Words piled high in her mouth, throwing themselves against the back of her teeth, trying to pry free into the air. But what they had seen and done held her mouth shut. It wasn't that she didn't want to talk to her friends; there was probably nothing she wanted more. But what could they say in the wake of battle that wouldn't sound trite?

They had all been there. They had all lived through it. Their hearts had hammered with expectation and slowed to accompany the monotony of conflict. The only thing worse than the silence, Brit knew, would be stilted, forced conversation. So she let her words go. The girls exchanged weary half-smiles, muttered goodnights, and slid beneath the covers of their beds.

Brit felt herself falling asleep. Sleep in-game was like taking sleeping pills. You find yourself drifting away from awakeness, your mind blinks, and then you sit up alert and rested hours later.

But while she had been cursed with the Sleep status, forced into that prolonged slumber, the machinery changed. Now she found herself falling asleep through determination, willing her mind to swim away from awakeness, toward the abstraction of dreams.

Dreams. They were new too. She thought about telling Suzanne and Mikayla after she had the first one, but she knew her friends too well. Suzanne would get that wounded, deer-in-headlights look she got whenever some feature in the game glitched. "But that's not how I programmed it!" She knew the exact shrillness that Suzanne's voice would take, the number of panicked breaths she'd inhale. No thanks. No need to worry her with something so small.

And she couldn't tell Mikayla . . . because she couldn't. Partially because of what the dreams were about and partially because the dreams allowed her some small measure of privacy. They offered her a vacation from Io, and she hoarded them like a dragon hoards gold.

*Are there dragons in this game?* Brit could feel herself slipping away. She closed her eyes and the dream took her.

At first it seemed less like a dream than a memory. Back on the craggy battlefield, her halberd in hand, her health bar full. Watching Mikayla cut through an enemy with those efficient little slashes she fought with. An enemy Monk charging straight at her.

Brit brought her halberd down, cleaving through armor. She feels the blow reverberate up the shaft of her halberd, through her arms into her body. It joins in the rhythm of her heart. Sometimes she loves the game.

But then she meets the eyes of the Monk and they are too deep, too well drawn. No monochromatic pupil floating in a sea of white. Flecked with color, drawn with the currents and pathos she knows from another world. The real world.

And above his head, his icon is green. She's gotten so used to the grey icons over the heads

211

of NPCs that she barely registers them anymore. But this Monk's icon is green. Like Mikayla's and Suzanne's. Like hers.

"No . . . " he says, his body already going through the mesmerizing process of pixelation. "I just wanted to get home." By the time he starts that last word, his body is gone. *Home* comes out as a puff of breeze, a whisper of a ghost.

Brit recoils in what feels like horror. She drops her halberd. She sees Mikayla cuff an enemy Ranger in the face with her shield. The Ranger staggers, lowering his guard. Mikayla sees the opening and drives her sword in up to the hilt.

Above the enemy Ranger's head the green icon flickers and disappears. The same human—*soulful*—eyes go dim. Mikayla pulls back her sword and there's blood. There's so much blood. How can a body be that full of anything when it's devoid of life?

The Ranger doesn't pixelate but falls prone. His face settles into an accusatory, pleading expression.

*Please.* But it's too late, no take backs. Brit knows they're playing for keeps.

She looks up at the army of Altairi charging at her. A cloud of green icons float over their heads. And their eyes—is that fear? Is it that same poison she feels pumping through her own veins, spreading to every bit of her? Infecting her limbs until she can no longer stand the battle or stand in general. She curls into a ball, goes fetal waiting for the end.

But then the scene changes and she isn't on the battlefield. She isn't in Pyxis, in Io. She's in Intro to Technology, waiting for Mr. Wells to come in.

She looks down. She's wearing some band's shirt and her favorite pair of jeans. She's five feet tall again. Her arms are her arms, not bulging with muscle, but pale and freckled. Black nail polish and the two-fingered peace sign ring. Some note to herself scribbled on the back of her left hand in pen.

The bell rings. Mr. Wells jogs into the room. "Well, Brit?" he asks. "Did you finish your project?"

"Yes," she says, although that must be a lie. He's staring at her, studying her face like he knows she's bullshitting. This is an unprecedented level of scrutiny from Mr. Wells.

"Well, you're presenting first." She stands, walks to the front of the room. Only then does she see the rest of her classmates. They're monsters. They're gargantulas and dire wolves, redcaps and rat kings. Coiled around a row of desks in the back is the Lamia, a pair of ridiculous thick-rimmed glasses obscuring her serpentine face.

"Are you ready?" Mr. Wells asks, but then he isn't Mr. Wells. He's Ramses leering down from his throne. The classroom is an arena. The monsters throw themselves on her, scratching and slashing, biting and gnawing.

"Are you ready?" Mr. Ramses repeats, his voice shaking with laughter. "Are you ready?" He's shouting the three words over and over until they too are just another assault, joining with the teeth and claws of the monsters. She feels her body ripped into nothing and looks down and her hands are not her hands but her character's, strong and unblemished, digitally rendered hands. Connected to arms not her own, a body not her own. There were no monsters. She bolted upright in her bed. She was awake, relatively speaking. Sighs. She throws herself back down onto the bed.

She wouldn't tell this dream to Mikayla and Suzanne either.